Creole

José Eduardo Agualusa was born in Huambo, Angola in 1960. For a number of years he lived in Lisbon and he now resides in Rio de Janeiro with his wife and young son.

Agualusa's first work of fiction, *The Conspiracy*, a historical novel set in Sao Paulo de Luanda between 1880 and 1911, paints a fascinating portrait of a society marked by opposites, in which only those who can adapt have any chance of success. Other novels include *The Market of the Damned* (1992) and *The Rainy Season*, which depicts the devastating history of an Angola tormented by thirty years of civil war.

José Eduardo Agualusa has also published a book of short stories and *At the Heart of the Forests*, a poetry collection. His novel *Creole*, which has evoked comparisons to Bruce Chatwin's *The Viceroy of Ouidah*, was awarded the Portuguese Grand Prize for Literature, and is a best-seller in Angola, Brazil, France, Germany, Italy, Portugal and Spain (including its Catalan translation). Agualusa's recent book, *Lisboa Africana*, produced in collaboration with Fernando Semedo and photographer Elza Rocha, is a much lauded volume about Lisbon's African Community.

Praise for *Creole:*

'I was very much impressed by *Creole* – a very readable, evocative, stylish work. I don't know of anything quite like it or anything written from that particular historical perspective – I loved the juxtapositions of decadent Europe and Africa, the literary references, and the contrasts of different superstitions. Also it seemed to me impeccably translated' – Margaret Drabble

'A compelling and impressive début . . . using poetic images and precisely crafted prose, *Creole* leads us across a European looking-glass into nineteenth-century Brazil and Africa, once isolated lands now beset by the cruelties of the slave trade'
– Richard Zimler, author of *The Last Kabbalist of Lisbon*

'One of the most powerful and most beautiful arguments against a stereotyped vision of Africa. Agualusa rediscovers the brutal and fascinating world of mulatto Africa, a world riddled with love and hate that jumps social barriers; with political riots that mobilize whites as well as blacks; and with intrigues that unfold in cosmopolitan settings. In short, a Creole nation that has needed more than a century to rebuild the beauty and the magnetism of this stolen memory'
– *El País*

Creole

JOSÉ EDUARDO AGUALUSA

Translated from the Portuguese
by Daniel Hahn

A

ARCADIA BOOKS
LONDON

Arcadia Books Ltd
15–16 Nassau Street
London W1W 7AB
www.arcadiabooks.co.uk

First published in the United Kingdom 2002
Originally published by Publicações Dom Quixote, Lisbon, 1997
Copyright © José Eduardo Agualusa 1997
English translation copyright © Daniel Hahn 2002

A catalogue record for this book is available from the British Library.

ISBN 1–900850–61–3

Typeset by Northern Phototypesetting Co. Ltd, Bolton
Printed by Bell & Bain, Glasgow

Acknowledgements
Arcadia Books acknowledges the financial support of the Instituto Camões,
Portugal and the Arts Council of England.

Arcadia Books distributors are as follows:

in the UK and elsewhere in Europe:
Turnaround Publishers Services
Unit 3, Olympia Trading Estate
Coburg Road
London N22 6TZ

in the USA and Canada:
Consortium Book Sales and Distribution
1045 Westgate Drive
St Paul, MN 55114-1065

in Australia:
Tower Books
PO Box 213
Brookvale, NSW 2100

in New Zealand:
Addenda
Box 78224
Grey Lynn
Auckland

in South Africa:
Quartet Sales and Marketing
PO Box 1218
Northcliffe
Johannesburg 2115

ANGOLA

Letter to Madame de Jouarre
Luanda, May 1868

My dear godmother,

Yesterday evening I disembarked at Luanda, carried on shore by two sailors from Cabinda. Hurled onto the beach, wet and humiliated, I was immediately assaulted by the alarming sensation of having left the real world behind me. I breathed in the hot, humid Angolan air, aware of the sweet scents of fruit and sugar-cane, and gradually began to recognize another smell, something subtler, more melancholy, not unlike the smell of death and decay. I think this is the smell that travellers refer to when they speak of Africa.

Looking at the city that rose wearily before me, I wondered whether perhaps it would have been better if I had not brought Smith. I watched him disembarking, trying to maintain his old-fashioned Scottish uprightness while riding two Negroes, his right leg over the left shoulder of one of them, his left over the right shoulder of the other. By the time he reached me, furious and dishevelled, he excused himself and vomited. 'Welcome to Portugal!' I said.

Around us was an agitated crowd of people, laughing and shouting, moving bundles, leading animals. Eventually Smith managed to engage two covered litters, and on we went, covered in salt and sweat, through a run of twisted, badly paved little streets. Groups of natives were talking in the shade of the walls, or sleeping stretched out, face down in the dust. In the doorway of the Hotel Glória an extraordinary figure awaited us, a man who seemed to be part-transformed from human into bird. An old man, tall, slim, with a thin face, a hooked nose and round, shining eyes:

'Your Excellency!' he shouted, proffering his hand. 'I am Colonel Arcénio de Carpo.'

I knew all about him. An Austrian scientist, a friend of mine, who had spent several years studying the flora and fauna in the bushlands of Angola, had spoken enthusiastically to me about him: 'In Luanda even the sun obeys him. Almost nothing happens in that city without the old man's say-so.' The rank of 'Colonel' which he flaunts so proudly – Colonel, Commander-in-Chief of the provinces of Bié, Bailundo and Embo (!) – has no actual meaning, however, other than as an honorary title, as Arcénio de Carpo is no military man, nor has he ever visited those provinces – provinces which in fact have no allegiance to the Portuguese government and – incidentally – none of which houses so much as a single regiment.

When he learned of my trip, my friend insisted on writing to Arcénio de Carpo. I don't know what he wrote, but I wouldn't be surprised if he had said that from the solitude of my palace in Paris I controlled the movement of the stars. For what I do know is that Arcénio welcomed me as though I were a prince:

'You gentlemen will stay with me,' he said, and pointing to the dark façade of the Glória, added 'This place isn't a hotel, it's a slave-camp.'

Arcénio Pompílio Pompeu de Carpo was born in Madeira, the child of travelling actors. Exiled to Angola for a crime of conscience (so he says) or perhaps for some real crime (for so mutter his enemies) he now lives up in

Cidade Alta, in a spacious two-floor colonial manor, the ground floor ringed by a broad wooden balcony. In the afternoons this balcony is protected from the sun with straw matting, which people here call *luandos*, or *luangos*, which makes it possible to keep the house cool throughout the day. As soon as we arrived, Arcénio sent a boy to my quarters to rub me down with sugar-cane rum, the only remedy (so he said) capable of preventing the diseases that come from contact with sea-water.

He then showed me the rest of the house, including the yard, a wide, deep area partly taken up by houses for his slaves, and his stores of ivory, rubber and wax. Fixed to the high walls were iron cages, and in the middle of the yard there was even a whipping-post which the Colonel assured me he had never used. It was not so long ago, however, that this place was being used to fatten up Negroes brought in from the interior, on their way out to Brazil.

Have you gathered then, my dear godmother, how Sr Arcénio de Carpo made his fortune? Exactly: by buying and selling wretched humanity. Or, as he prefers to put it, 'by contributing to the growth of Brazil'. And if you believe what is said in Luanda, he's still working tirelessly for that same growth. 'The English must never see me defeated,' he declared, excited, when I asked him if the trafficking of Negroes still went on in the colony.

The Colonel believes that the emancipation movement has been secretly financed by the British and North Americans, who are hoping to prevent the consolidation of a strong power in South America: 'English America is over-populated. Every year millions of European farmers make their way into the interior there. So it's easy for them to be all humanistic and raise their voices against slavery. But Brazil, where the number of European settlers is far fewer, depends entirely on slaves. If the slave trade were to stop, Brazilian agriculture would simply disintegrate. At the same time England means to ruin the élites which could rule Angola tomorrow; you can see the real proof of this double-dealing in the fact that the British navy doesn't only capture and sink slave-ships, but has been doing the same to vessels carrying cargo from all kinds of different trades.'

Arcénio's hatred of the English has grown considerably since an incident that to this day the Luandans still laugh about. A few years ago the old settler had the audacity to invite the captain of the British cruiser *Water-Witch*, responsible for guarding Africa's Western coastline, to lunch on one of his own ships – the *Herói dos Mares*, the 'Hero of the Seas'. Once the meal was done he turned to the Englishman and asked him, smiling, whether he was planning to take action against that very same ship:

'This very night, or tomorrow at the latest, this ship will leave Luanda for the north-east of Brazil, with 400 slaves in its cellars.'

The English captain laughed at Arcénio's joke, and in the same light-hearted tone replied that he would do everything he could to stop it. The very next day he invited Arcénio for lunch on the *Water-Witch*, and, the meal over, informed him that the *Herói dos Mares* had been captured and sent to Sierra Leone.

In Senhor Arcénio's absolute logic, condemning slavery is a sign of bowing down before English arrogance, and supporting the emancipation societies an act of treachery. And what is one to think of those Deputies back home who go to court to defend the greater participation of our own navy in the international fleet sent to guard Africa's seas? Arcénio has no doubt:

'What to think of them? Excellency, there is so little substance to the Portuguese people today, you could even fit them all in Portugal!'

And as for the Portuguese of yesteryear, from the old stock of Cabral, Camões and Fernão Mendes Pinto, there are, I think, only two left, my dear godmother – he and I.

Your godson,
Fradique

Letter to Madame de Jouarre
Luanda, June 1868

My dear godmother,

Still in Luanda, living as the guest of Sr Arcénio de Carpo, just wandering around, putting on weight. Smith, meanwhile, is just putting on weight. Surprisingly (or perhaps not so surprisingly) he has become a convert to hot Angolan food, and is often to be found among the servants, happily eating *funge* and beans. In this company he picks up the news from the city, so even here in Angola I can 'read Smith' every morning. No, so I don't know the exact price of gold on the London Stock Exchange, I don't know where Livingstone is headed, nor am I able to follow the intrigues at court. But to make up for this I do know that roasted rats are still selling very well in Luanda's markets, at fifteen *réis* a dozen, wooden skewers through their stomachs, and that there have been disturbances in Sumbe and the Congo.

While I soap my face and sharpen my razor, Smith also tells me of the little domestic dramas with which the imaginations of the Luandans are so richly fed. If I am to believe what I have heard, there is not a single honest man in this city, nor one faithful wife or modest young girl. In general the settlers can be divided into:

(1) Criminals serving out their time in exile
(2) Exiles who have served their time, but wisely choose to stick around.

As for the children-of-the-country, a euphemism which certain mulattos and free Negroes use to refer to themselves, they spend their time in the city's coffee-houses studiously fabricating intrigues, something they have a great gift for doing. Unfortunately, while they destroy each other for some tiny job in the Treasury hierarchy, the exiles seduce their wives and daughters, steal their lands and businesses, and strengthen their own power in the administration of the colony.

As for work, well, no one in Luanda does any work but the slaves, and outside the city the so-called 'ignorant Negroes'. So for a Luandan work represents something inferior, unhealthy, something done by savages and prisoners. I've heard people at a shady café table mutter venomously: 'So-and-so comes from a working family.' The insinuation is cruel and capable of destroying reputations, because it suggests that the victim has only recently bought his first pair of shoes[1] and is probably a descendant of slaves.

(So it could be said that the Luandans, a classical people, understand their word for work, *trabalhar*, in its original sense, from the Latin *tripaliare*, that is, being martyred on a *tripaliu*. Which reminds me, did you know that the English word 'slave' comes from 'Slav', as the Slavs were the first Roman slaves? And of course there's also the Russian word *rabota*, which means 'work', and has as its root the word *rab*, 'slave'.)

'The mulattos', Arcénio confided in me, 'despise all the people from the interior because they work, and despise them still more because being black they want to go on doing it.' I was able to find proof of this theory right here in the house of my host. Arcénio has one son, a young man with the same name, tall and slim like his father, with prominent cheekbones and almond-shaped eyes, a long, curved moustache in the Romantic style; it is he who has really managed his father's fortune since it became almost impossible to carry on trading Negroes to

---

1 Slaves traditionally walked barefoot; shoes were a sign of being granted one's liberty – DH.

Brazil. Both he and his mother, Joana Benvindo, a coal-black lady from Benguela whom the old settler treats with the greatest respect (almost terror), live in the mansion in Cidade Alta. At supper, a meal served rather grandly in the cool hall on the ground floor, the young man sits on his father's left and gets into animated discussion with him about something or other. Intelligent, well informed and well spoken, he nonetheless prefers politics to philosophy, slanderous gossip to literature. According to him the blacks from the bushlands are a great obstacle to Angola's swift transformation into a modern country, as they have no concept of the State, they refuse to speak Portuguese and are still in thrall to all kinds of beliefs and superstitions.

I pointed out that the English, French and Germans also refuse to speak Portuguese, and reminded him that the Queen of Spain believes in the purifying powers of sweat from a nun's undergarments. And, after all, what's the difference between an African fetish stuck through with nails and a statue of a man nailed to a cross? Before he tries to make an African change his leopard-skin for a Poole tailcoat, or put on a pair of Malmstrom boots, he would do well to try to understand the world he's living in here and its philosophy!

The young Arcénio de Carpo looked at me with something between shock and disgust: 'Philosophy? So Your Excellency has come to Africa to look for philosophy?!' I nodded. Like many Europeans, he acts as though anything he doesn't know about can't possibly exist.

The contempt that the children-of-the-country feel for the people of the interior can be even better illustrated with a story that Smith told me. Two years ago, one of the richest businessmen and slave-owners in the country, a black man by the name of Senhor Mateus Lamartine, discovered that his only daughter, Carolina, was secretly corresponding with a young nurse, himself also a Negro, but one who had no connection with Luanda's old families. In a rage, he sent the young man a message summoning him to come at once. 'My dear young man,' he said when they were finally face to face. 'I have nothing against you, quite the opposite, I just don't want you as my son-in-law. I wouldn't refuse my daughter's hand to a poor white man, so long as he wasn't a convict, nor to a mulatto, so long as he had a handsome fortune. But for someone like you to marry Carolina you'd have to be the Emperor of Abyssinia.'

In despair the young man kidnapped his girlfriend and carried her off, up the river Quanza, to Feira do Dondo where he had family. That month a priest well respected throughout the bushlands, Nicolau dos Anjos, was visiting the village and agreed to marry the two fugitives on condition that they return to Luanda to ask the bride's father his pardon. This turned out to be bad advice: no sooner had the schooner arrived, while they were still on the quay, than a man pushed the nurse roughly, and when he turned to protest stabbed him in the throat and fled. A few weeks later Carolina was led to the *Igreja dos Remédios* church for a second wedding, on the strong arm of her father. Many recognized the groom, L.A., a professional hunter, a Minhoto from Braga, the murderer himself.

That night Carolina killed her husband. The Chief of Police, himself a friend of the nurse's, didn't need to question her: 'It was an accident. Senhor L.A. was cleaning his Winchester rifle, as he did every night, when it went off. The bullet went into his chin and came out at the nape of his neck.'

This is where our fierce Camilo would have ended his story. Zola would have ended his earlier still, on the quay where the first blood was spilt. But the crazy Gods of Africa gave it an impossible ending. Do you want to know what happened? Seven months later Carolina gave birth to a black boy. The child didn't cry when the midwife lifted him into her arms and carried him out into the night to show him the stars, the dark trees, and everything still and everything moving where the spirits of the past keep hidden, keeping watch.

He didn't cry. With a loud, clear voice, his father's voice, he denounced his slaving grandfather. He did the same in the presence of several witnesses, explaining that the old man had contracted L.A. and that the two had planned the crime together. Then he fell silent, and at last began to cry, just as all children cry when they notice the world for the first time.

Old Mateus Lamartine committed suicide last week.

Your loving godson,
Fradique

Letter to Madame de Jouarre
Luanda, June 1868

My dear godmother,

Finding myself today rather more reconciled to the human race, I'll return to its company with the complete account of what I've seen and done beneath these wide African skies.

On Sunday I was invited to the Governor's Ball, an event of great splendour, noise and show, where one tends to find *toute Luanda* – that is, anyone in this city who, having a bit of capital, knows how to read and write. In the halls of the palace you can see honest traders mixing with exiled criminals, children-of-the-country with blond European adventurers, slave-owners with abolitionists, monarchists with republicans, priests with masons. After all, some of the most prosperous business-men from São Paolo de Luanda began their fortunes asking for loans of a few copper *macutas* with which they could buy fish to fry, then selling them at the fairs and markets. It wasn't long before their *macutas* became ten-cent *tostões*, then pounds, before ending up as thousands of *réis*.

It's hard to imagine a more interesting collection of physical and psychological types, even pathological types, gathered under the same roof. Of all these people it is the figure of Senhora Gabriela Santamarinha that stands out. The people of Luanda, who claim superiority in all things, and for whom every excess is a virtue, have assured me – with great seriousness – that this lady is the ugliest in the world. And I, who have travelled the world over (give or take a little), I am forced to agree. There is not, there cannot be, a woman so thoroughly ugly who is so content to be so. Seeing her reminded me of some lines from the Brazilian poet Gregório de Matos,

describing a Creole Negress: 'A mouth drawn so wide /
That the teeth / Wander around it / In a state of agita-
tion'. Gabriela Santamarinha is of a natural ugliness,
without any artifice or rhetoric, and she exercises it in
every gesture, every sentence, in her smell, in the bestial
way in which she walks. 'Look how ugly she is!' an
excited Arcénio de Carpo said to me; 'there's never been
a creature like her, not even among the aboriginals of
Australia.'

'Not even in London's freak-shows!' I agreed, shocked,
my eyes fixed on the dreadful figure.

'They call her the Damned Mouth', the Colonel
explained, 'the Spitting Mouth, the Murderous Mouth or
the Rotten Mouth. They say that birds die of disgust as
she passes.'

They also say (and Arcénio swears this is true) that
Gabriela Santamarinha was found, a baby just a few days
old, in a public lavatory, and raised by a Galician priest
who gave her his name and from whom she inherited two
estates in the *musseques*, the outskirts of town. 'But she
never lost her original stench, and that's why they also
call her the Abominable Monster of the Lavatories,'
Arcénio said, motioning to take my arm.

'Come, I'll introduce you.'

I recoiled in horror. 'God, there's really no need . . .'

Arcénio de Carpo then explained to me that being
introduced to Gabriela Santamarinha is practically a rite
of initiation in Luanda. 'A lot of people around here are
betting that Your Excellency will lose his nerve,' he said.
'Take a deep breath and come with me. Don't breathe
when you're up close.'

Gabriela Santamarinha seemed to be waiting for that
moment. She gave a slight bow, and while I pretended to
kiss her fingers, which were covered in thick gold rings,
she spat her poison:

'I've heard that you go everywhere in the company of an English slave,' she said, making me catch my breath. 'At my place I only have albino slave-girls, and I've heard that in Brazil one can get white or almost-white slaves at a good price. But I didn't know there was still slavery in Europe. Won't you sell me yours?'

I moved away, tormented by the certainty that that night was going to be one of the worst in my life. It wasn't. The very next moment I saw her: the most beautiful woman in the world. They were dancing the *rebita*, a fashionable dance which combines a rare harmony with the worldly grace of the waltz and wild African rhythms. The Master of Ceremonies, a black officer known as Gingão, was leading the dance in a mysterious language which they later assured me was actually French.

When I saw her – the most beautiful woman in the world – at that very moment I was reconciled to humanity, and my eyes opened with a new interest in this country and its peoples.

There have been moments in my life – dusk falling on the Alps, an evening in Asmera when I surprised a jaguar, right in front of me, ready to pounce – there have been moments which have made me feel the proof of God; that is, of Life. Maybe that is what Buddhists call Nirvana. When I first saw her I felt the very same emotion.

She danced, but 'dance' is an inadequate word, she was magnificent, spinning the rounds of the *rebita*, ornate fabrics curving over her breast, her hair tall and intricately dressed, a fine gold chain clasped, dazzling, around her dark gazelle-like neck. For a second she held my gaze with the warm glow of her black eyes, then she disappeared.

Arcénio de Carpo must have noticed my distress. Lowering his voice and taking me by the arm, with the intimacy of an old comrade, he led me out on to the verandah.

'God is a democrat,' he said. 'A democrat and a social-
ist. Take the case of Dona Ana Olímpia. She was born in
this city, the daughter of a slave, and today she's one of
the richest women in the country, herself mistress to
many slaves, powerful and respected.'

It's a curious story. As I said, Ana Olímpia was born a
slave. Her father, however, was a Congolese prince who
spent many years rotting away in a flooded cell in Fort-
aleza do Penedo, north of Luanda. Lured into an ambush
by the Portuguese soldiers he was taken prisoner,
together with all those accompanying him, including
three of his wives. Once a month they would take the
Prince in a procession to the Governor's Palace, in his
general's uniform, so that the Negroes would see him and
believe he was being well treated.

'He was an admirable man,' recalled Arcénio de Carpo.
'He would talk to us in good Portuguese, as equal to
equal, protesting against his imprisonment, which he
considered illegal (and which indeed it was), and
demanding redress. When he passed by on his way to the
Palace, huge and majestic among the garrison from the
fort, the people would throw themselves to the ground
and cover their heads with sand – nobody dared look him
in the eye. Every month the Governor assured him that he
would soon be freed, expressing his regret at the situation, but knowing full well that the Prince would die in
prison.' Arcénio also remembered what became of the
three women. 'They were sold as slaves. I bought two of
them, and the third, who was pregnant, was taken by Victorino Vaz de Caminha.'

Victorino Vaz de Caminha, a very peculiar old man,
took the pregnant woman as his cook, and fourteen years
later, after the death of the Congolese Prince, married the
daughter, Ana Olímpia. Talking to her I was astonished to

hear her quoting Kant and Confucius, ridiculing Charles Darwin's theories, and making intelligent and original comments on the modern French lyric. I asked her 'What is a woman like you doing somewhere like this?'

She smiled, ravishingly: 'This place is my country.'

A country which surprises me every day.

Your almost-African godson,
Fradique

Letter to Ana Olímpia
Benguela, May 1872

My dear friend,

Until last week I considered myself if not exactly immortal, then at least immune to the common ills that afflict mankind. Over the last twenty years I have passed unharmed through the drunken nights of Coimbra, the Abyssinian War, Iceland and the Sahara; I dared even to frequent São Bento when the prolixity of Parliament was at its height, and always managed to escape from these excesses and adventures without coming to any harm. And now here I am in Benguela, since last week confined to my bed and burning up with fever.

The friend in whose house I'm a guest, one of this city's doctors, assures me that I will live. Luís Gonzaga was my fellow-student in Coimbra. The force of his laughter, which shook the chandeliers and startled the birds, made him popular among the students, as did his gift for playing the guitar. Happy, irresponsible, more often to be found in a tavern than buried in a textbook, it took him almost ten years to complete his course. Then he set off for Africa and set up in Benguela. Why Benguela? We've talked a lot over the past few days, but I haven't been able to get an answer to that question.

We have been thinking about Coimbra, I more than he as he seems to have lost interest in anything to do with the old Portugal. The kind of open-air enclosure he's living in has made him a different man. He listens a lot, he talks less, he still laughs but less outrageously, and when he takes the guitar in his arms it is to create melodies unlike anything I've heard before, contaminated with the same sunny melancholy (if that makes any sense) that is burying this whole city.

Sometimes I hear him speaking in Umbundu to the

cook, António Salvador, a wise man who between 1854 and 1856 accompanied David Livingstone on that famous expedition which discovered the Victoria Falls. By now the two seem to be compatriots, for not only does Luís Gonzaga speak the old man's language, he speaks it like an Ovimbundu. He laughs with his old energy again, he gestures wildly, claps his hands, and as I watch him he seems to have been colonized by this country.

At his own expense my friend has set up a little hospital, in the Rua da Quitanda, which treats soldiers, exiles and poor blacks almost exclusively, since the well-off and all the European settlers get their treatment at home. Luís Gonzaga does what he can to look after everybody. When he lacks the means or the knowledge, he gathers six of his men, instals the patient in a litter or on a hammock hung between two horses, and the little expedition sets off through the bush, fifteen or twenty kilometres, until they reach a tall, round rock at whose foot they find a witchdoctor at worship.

I imagine none of this is new to you. I am beginning to understand that everywhere that is still dominated by the night, that is, in every place which has not yet seen the arrival of electric lighting, there are no exact sciences. What there is instead is the great darkness that follows the setting of the sun, the high skies in which stars navigate. Rumours and fear. Dancing spirits. And they are all just so many un-explanations.

Writing all this makes me think that you must be wanting to know whether I have in fact been able to throw any light on the strange murmuring which brought me here. Unfortunately not – I hear it just the same in these bushlands, but vague and confused like the weary telling of a dream.

In the state I am in, these things seem all the more fantastic. Stretched out in bed, at once with a blazing fever and shivering with cold, I try to understand the secrets of Africa. And I think about you. I think about you a lot. In my disorganized soul the image of you somehow serves to make things clear and revive me. If I survive, can I encourage a hope of seeing you again in Luanda?

Write, say yes, certain in the knowledge that only your words will make me better (Luís Gonzaga is threatening to take me to the witchdoctor!).

Your loving friend,
Fradique

Letter to Eça de Queiroz
Luanda, August 1872

My dear friend,

I found your letter when I arrived back from the bush-lands of Benguela, where I'd been out seeking confirmation of an extraordinary local rumour. I didn't succeed, as it happens, but I was able to witness an event out of which I'm sure you with a few quick lines could easily create a work of literature. I, being rather more impoverished, will simply relate the story as it took place:

A week ago an exile by the name (or nickname, which is much the same here) of João Bacalhau[2] stabbed another settler and believing him to be dead fled into the bush. It was already dark. Bacalhau, who only came in from Portugal a few weeks ago and knew little of the country, went deeper and deeper into the thick, rustling darkness of Africa with growing dread. His hands out in front of him, panting, tripping this way and falling that, he kept running until he could no longer feel anything at all – not tiredness, not fear, not pain – until it seemed to him that his body and his soul had been parted. Then he leaned up against the big trunk of a mango tree and fell asleep.

He awoke with the first lights of morning, with the sudden silence of the birds. There was something moving beyond the grove of trees. Something creeping up the hill, getting closer, numerous and determined. In panic, Bacalhau climbed up the tree, and from there looked down at the strange procession approaching him.

There were some twenty men. Father Nicolau dos Anjos was leading them, holding tightly on to a long ivory cross. I was just behind him, with a doctor friend, Luís Gonzaga, in whose house I was staying, and an army

2 Literally, 'John Salt-Cod' – DH.

lieutenant, a pale, anxious young man, to whom I had frequently to offer my arm in order to stop him fainting.
Behind us there were servants shaking little bells, holding up lighted candles, their magnificent deep copper
voices raised, singing hymns of glory to the Lord.

It isn't hard to imagine João Bacalhau's alarm when he
saw the procession stop, surrounding the mango tree,
and the terrible face of the canon raised up towards him.
I think I've already spoken about Nicolau dos Anjos in my
earlier letters. He is one of Angola's most interesting figures, and you hear his name spoken everywhere you go.
Not long after my arrival, for instance, I heard the head of
the Bengo Council putting an end to a heated theological
discussion quoting the priest:

'The ideas of rulers and their people change with the
corruption of the centuries, but both are dominated by
God's laws, which are eternal and unchanging. Science
has killed the idea of God; it is now up to science to revive
it.'

Later on, a local *pombeiro*, a sort of travelling trader, told
me the confused tale of a hippopotamus hunt. As far as I
could tell, one of the hunters, who had been wounded in
the stomach when his own gun went off accidentally, was
lying out on the grass, dead or waiting to die. But then
who should appear but Nicolau dos Anjos: 'You are
cured,' he said, passing his right hand over the body of
the unfortunate man. 'Rise up and return home.' The
hunter did as he was told (it is hard not to obey an order
from the priest); he got up and made his way into the city,
where he arrived quite fully alive.

And this great man, so feared and respected, is a dwarf!
His head, stuck on a tiny child's trunk, seems enormous,
much bigger than a normal man's. But there is such
authority emanating from him, especially when he
speaks, that few people manage to attain greater stature

than he does. Rough, crude, often dogmatic, the priest is nonetheless a great conversationalist. It gives me enormous pleasure to look back on the long hours we spent – he and I and Luís Gonzaga – arguing about the decline in spirituality and the triumph of materialism in this century of ours:

'You gentlemen are trying to exile God from the Universe,' the holy man would complain. 'The barricade, the guillotine, the "International", the people's proclamations against power, these are all appalling symptoms afflicting the modern age. Our century has given itself up to the Hydra of Revolution just as Ajax did himself to the raging Eumenides in that ancient tragedy.'

He would say these fierce things seated in the consoling shade of a bower of bougainvillea, drinking German beer, while all around us Benguela dozed under the midday sun. My friend, smiling, pointed out to him that the modern age was 7,000 kilometres away. 'It's going to take it some time yet to get here.'

'No,' replied the priest, pointing at me; 'it's here already.'

But to return to João Bacalhau. It was, as I was saying, with some alarm that he saw us surround the tree: twenty men and a tiny black priest. The dark earth, the tall trees, the resonant chanting, the candles and the cross, all filled him with wonder and fear.

He saw the priest look up and give the order: 'Get up there and bring him down . . .'

'No! Don't come up!' Bacalhau shouted. 'Don't come up – I'll come right down.'

Down on the ground everyone began shouting and running about. Only the priest and I remained. It was only then that we were able to make out high up among the leaves the livid face of João Bacalhau, and it was only then that Bacalhau noticed the blue face, right next to his own, of the sad slave who had hanged himself there and whose body we had at last come to recover.

Down on the ground Nicolau dos Anjos just muttered 'My, my . . .'.

And I, who for a few seconds had believed myself to have been a witness to a terrifying phenomenon, muttered myself, 'My, my . . .'.

Luís Gonzaga and I had to get João Bacalhau down from the tree and take him into the town where at nightfall he made peace with the other settler, who for his part had suffered nothing worse than a wound in his arm.

Of the men in the procession, two or three ran off into the bush and were never seen again. And doubtless they are even now astonishing the masses with tales of another of Nicolau dos Anjos' miracles.

And there, my dear José Maria, you can see how myths are born.

Your faithful friend,
Fradique

Letter to Madame de Jouarre
Luanda, August 1872

My dear godmother,

Doubtless you remember Madame Kirkowitz? In fact I think it was at one of those famous winter salons at your house that she came out with that memorable statement of hers: 'Black women have something poisonous in their blood, something which first enslaves then atrophies and destroys the hearts of white men.' I remember how people laughed and protested, but I took her very seriously – I realized that behind those few words of hers were years and years of merciless scientific observation. I have no doubt that during her long years living in Brazil the sad old widow saw dozens of gentlemen dying in the arms of their black mistresses; I now know that one of these gentlemen was her husband.

Back in Luanda I often remember this resentful theory, and the cold, pale, bitter image of Madame Kirkowitz comes back to me. I didn't choose those three adjectives thoughtlessly, by the way; a few days ago, talking about the few European women living in Luanda, Arcénio de Carpo Jr asked me: 'Have you noticed that those things we appreciate in a beer we consider faults in a woman?' Those cold, bitter women so like Madame Kirkowitz even go so far as to share her hatred for black and mulatto women. 'Black women are a terrible evil,' the English consul's wife confided to me one evening, 'but the mulatto women are even worse; not only do they pursue married men but they also laugh at us, and despise us too.'

I do think that there's an element of truth in her complaint. I recently saw an amateur production of *Othello*, the Shakespeare play, at the Providência Theatre. Three magnificent women, three bronze flowers (to use an imperfect metaphor popular with the local troubadours), dominated the little audience effortlessly. They laughed amongst themselves, and it was obvious that they were enjoying the outrage of their own beauty. The English consul's wife greeted me at a distance, with a dull smile; later I watched her leave the room in floods of tears, supported on her husband's arm, long before Desdemona was to be killed by the Moor. As he left, the consul cast a quick glance back towards the three graces, and it wasn't hard for me to guess at the intrigue.

On another occasion I was chatting with old Arcénio de Carpo, after supper, in the two hours he reserves for what he calls his 'smoking ceremony'. There is usually a young mulatto woman sitting behind my host, with honey-coloured eyes, oriental features and a sweet name – Lúcia – to whom some years ago the Colonel had offered her freedom. Whenever he finishes a cigarette Lúcia lights another for him, inhaling on it at some length, tenderly, before passing it over to him. (For me, she just passes over the matches!)

That night the topic of the conversation was feminine beauty.

'Danger attracts men, and that's why men are attracted to women,' the Colonel was theorizing. 'Women are the most dangerous breed in all creation. Of course, I'm not talking about women from Paris or Lisbon or even women from Rome. I'm talking about Woman, dammit, the whole, real woman.'

Lúcia smiled triumphantly.

'European women', the Colonel continued, 'are to African women what boiled chicken is to a barbecue. They're missing all the colour, the scent, the flavour, the warmth. They're missing the pepper, my friend. They're missing the soul.'

Lúcia lit another cigarette. She didn't say a word. She just lit the cigarette and looked me in the eye as she inhaled its smoke.

Since I've been here I've also renewed my acquaintance with another daughter-of-the-country, a lady by the name of Ana Olímpia, by whom I was greatly struck four years ago. Her husband died a few months back in the wreck of a pilot-boat. Victorino Vaz de Caminha, as he was called, was a remarkable man, who was born in Bahia but after Brazil's independence chose to remain Portuguese here in Angola. He was tall, slim with a long face, a very wild, very white beard which cascaded down over his chest, an excessive, contradictory character, whom I heard defending slavery and libertarian revolution at the same time and with just the same degree of fervour. The owner of three slaving ships, he knew exactly what he wanted to name them: Liberty, Equality and Fraternity.

As a slave-trader he made a great fortune and earned himself considerable respect across the country. As an anarchist he put his name to some half-dozen anti-clerical pamphlets, then was married in the Church of Nossa Senhora do Carmo; his bride, Ana Olímpia, was only fourteen at the time, and was (or had been) his slave.

The ceremony, which was deliberately luxurious, divided Luanda's little society between rage and astonishment. Father Nicolau dos Anjos still shudders to remember it: 'Victorino Vaz de Caminha was the Devil Himself,' he told me in Benguela. 'He put on that expensive spectacle just to ridicule the church and mock society.'

I believe that he did it for love.

Aged sixty-something, his liver ruined by the waters of Africa and the strong *cachaça* of Brazil, he didn't expect to live long. And from that day on he lived only for Ana Olímpia. He sent for a French teacher from Paris, who during his twelve months in Luanda managed to get twelve slave-girls pregnant. Impressed at the Frenchman's stamina, and naturally at the same time somewhat concerned, the old anarchist wanted to be sure that there

would not be a similar episode with the music teacher. So
he went to Naples himself, and there found a delicate,
perfumed, affected young man, whom the Luandans
would come to call *Ohali*, the Crested Grebe. Only those
who had seen this beautiful bird – with his flaming costume hat, his red bow, his black morning-coat and white
gloves – only those who had seen him walking, vain and
feminine, across the fields of southern Angola, could
understand how well such a nickname suited the Italian.

Ohali never returned home, and when I arrived back I
found him here still, giving piano lessons to the ladies of
Luanda, trading in perfumes, planning parties. He lost his
voice following a strange fever, but used this deficiency to
his advantage acting as prompter for the entertainments
at the Providência Theatre. I saw him (or, rather, heard
him) acting a few times, whispering with superiority, and
it was only then that I understood why so many of the
self-styled actors in this country speak with an undis-
guised Neapolitan accent.

Beside all these precious ways of passing the time,
Ohali also keeps himself busy with the new art of photography. He has set up a little studio in the Rua Direita
do Bungo and there takes portraits of ladies and gentlemen of the colony, young men and women, assorted typ-
ical characters, all posing – alarmed or confused – in front
of a picture of Vesuvius belching fire.

A traveller recently arrived in Luanda might suppose,
from visiting a few houses, that the whole town had in
fact been to Italy. In my host's large dining-room, guarded
by two fierce rhinoceros heads, is the photo of Arcénio de
Carpo senior, sitting in a swinging chair, and standing to
his right, all in white, Arcénio de Carpo junior. In the
background the volcano is erupting. I've also seen a
jolly Gabriela Santamarinha smiling as Vesuvius engulfs
Pompeii. And in Ohali's studio I have even witnessed – I

swear this is true! – two litter-bearers, in loincloths, posing in front of the historic disaster, looking utterly astonished.

Victorino Vaz de Caminha was particularly concerned with his young wife's political, philosophical and literary education. He discussed Proudhon and Mikhail Alexandrovich Bakunin with her, and then gave her the inevitable Hugo to read, as well as the dreadful Baudelaire, brilliant Flaubert, our dear old Gautier, the vast, chaotic Balzac, and even the unbearable Lamartine, as well as Taine, Goncourt and Michelet. The bold child read them all, survived them, and became a strong, bright woman with opinions; in short, a woman with qualities hard to find even in a man!

I should add that Ana Olímpia doesn't merely discuss the origin of the species, or the latest happenings in Europe, as if she had always lived at the centre of the world; but she shows just as much interest studying the past of her own people, she collects legends and proverbs from various Angolan tribes, and is even putting together a Portuguese-Quimbundu dictionary. Once a year she travels to the northern provinces, the provinces which were once her father's, and the tribal chiefs and their elders seek her counsel. Wherever she is, whether on horseback amid a group of hunters, in a ballroom, or at home, surrounded by festive young black girls, her presence seems to attract the light.

Every Sunday evening, the mansion which she inherited from her husband brings together original, concerned and cultured young people, who discuss everything and question everything. I went to some of those meetings myself, and was impressed to see whites, blacks and half-castes, all united in their love for Angola. Ana Olímpia receives all her guests seated on a tall wicker chair, surrounded by her girls who keep her cool by waving light sandalwood fans, and who in all things serve her quickly and graciously.

The slavery issue is always a matter for excited debate at these salons, in which few defend the old system and the great majority fight for abolition; many of these latter come from households where slavery is very much in evidence, and almost all are children of businessmen implicated in the slave trade. Ana Olímpia, for example, following her husband's death did sell the three ships with which Victorino Vaz de Caminha had made his fortune, but only freed those workers in the fields and not her domestic slaves. I should point out, though, that native Luandans tend to be less cruel than the Portuguese. This being the case, when a slave has done something seriously wrong Ana Olímpia prefers not to punish them but to sell them – for in truth this is the worst punishment of all.

Gabriela Santamarinha, on the other hand, enjoys a reputation for brutality which is well deserved. I once saw her myself punishing a wretched young girl, beating her on the back of the hands with a strap, and so violently that blood spurted out, staining her dress. Then the young thing was tied to a post, completely naked, and Gabriela marked her back with blows from a switch. And her crime? She had allowed one of the little trained monkeys to escape, one of those creatures with which that dreadful character would entertain her guests (dressing them up in finery: the males in bow tie, waistcoat and top hat, the females in fabrics from the coast, and making them dance the fashionable *modas* of the country).

Father Nicolau dos Anjos, who would often stay in her house when he visited Luanda, said he was kept awake by the noise of the slave-girls' wailing: 'Every night she would select two or three albino girls, on some trivial pretext, and take the whip to them. I found this so inhuman that I raised the matter with her, and from that night I never heard the slaves screaming again. I later learnt that she hadn't stopped beating them, but had just taken to gagging them first!'

By freeing the workers from her farms Ana Olímpia managed to demonstrate one of the main theories of the emancipation movement, namely that a man will always work more and better if he is free, the payment of his wage being compensated for by the increased harvest. In a sugar plantation which she owns in Icolo e Bengo, Ana Olímpia was able to make 125,000 francs from a single harvest, ten times more than she had done when all the workers were slaves.

So why didn't she free her household slaves? 'Because' she said to me 'it would be like letting my own family go.' Later on I heard this same argument (which frankly I can't understand) from other Luandans: 'We have responsibilities to them,' Arcénio de Carpo junior once tried to explain to me. 'We can't set them free, as the wretches wouldn't know what to do with their freedom.'

To tell you the truth, I wouldn't really mind being Ana Olímpia's slave. Does that surprise you? I fear that as you read this you are already thinking about Madame Kirkowitz's appalling judgement. As I said, I think about her a great deal too.

Saudades,[3] from your godson,
Fradique

---

3 *Saudades* is one of the most frequently used of Portuguese words, and one of the least translatable. With a meaning that combines nostalgia, longing, homesickness and melancholy, a sense of missing places or people intensely, it is very commonly found in songs and poems, as well as being used, as here, as an affectionate signing-off in personal letters – DH.

EUROPE

Letter to Ana Olímpia
Paris, December 1872

My sweet Princess,

It is December in Paris. It was already December when I set out from Luanda, leaving the radiance of your gaze behind me. And it will be December yet, even after the month is over, and then will come only more December and winter, and December again and always the same, until I come back to the Sunny Season, and the land which is lit everywhere, always, by your gaze.

It is very December in Paris. After three weeks of snow and cold the waters of the Seine have thawed, swollen, and like a huge enraged serpent – perhaps Muene-Zambi-dia-Menha, the water divinity you've talked to me so much about – the river swept over the city, tearing down bridges, tearing up trees, attacking houses, buildings and national monuments.

The fog covers everything like a white night. At the height of the day the carriages go around with their lamps lit, while on the corners policemen stand with torches, showing their poor shipwrecked people the way. Beside the Arc de Triomphe, where twelve great boulevards come together, tall bonfires have been lit, but nobody more than a couple of hundred metres away can see them. The coachmen get lost in the mist and roam the city like ghosts, their passengers screaming and their horses running mad, and there have been carriages falling into the river and others smashing into trees or buildings.

In this night-struck city I am guided and comforted by the memory of your light. I see you, I see you constantly, just as I first saw you, so beautiful as you spun in the rounds of the *rebita*, or in serious contemplation in Muxima, alone in the chapel, while outside the still river under the wide sun, the solemn landscape, the flawless sky, seemed in silence to be meditating with you. Then I see you crossing the Veados Beach at a gallop. I watch you laughing in the distance and your laugh is carried over to me on the breeze, salty and fresh, humid and strong, and again I feel – as I felt then – a living presence, the presence of Life.

When you asked me, breathless, breathing the same air I was breathing, 'And what now?' I didn't know what to say. Three months later and I still don't know the answer. I've been a nomad my whole life. I've crossed half the world, from Chicago to Palestine, Iceland to the Sahara, and I've never known what name to give this anxious wandering. Now I know that I was looking for you. I know now that you are my destiny, my country, my church. I know that it became December when I left Luanda, and that ever since then Winter has been prowling like a ravenous wolf all around me.

Darwin claims that men descended from monkeys, and I'm sure that's just what happened in most cases – they did indeed 'descend'. But I feel the opposite must have happened in my family, which has rather been raised up from that original instead, raised up to the simple Portuguese. Then came Alfonso Henriques, generations of sailors and navigators, the Azores were discovered and peopled, and I was born. From this whole oceanic breed I do have one cousin left, Crazy André, who for many years has been in the northern seas running a brig set up to tackle the complicated business of cod-fishing.

I travelled with him in the autumn of 1850 (I like to think that when you were born I was crossing the white murmuring of the seas of Greenland) and had the chance to get to know his soul, developed through the nature in which he lives, and in imitation of it – cold and rough, wild even, but also generous and pure. One night a mutiny broke out on board (I can't now remember what brutality or injustice had occurred to cause this) and the sailors tied him up and took control of the boat. While they were deciding what to do with him – opinion was split between tossing him into the sea and giving him a good thrashing – they laid him out over a bulwark. The discussion dragged on, two, three hours, until finally André let out a great shout: 'Either in or out, idlers! Just not here as my back is starting to hurt!'

Are you wondering why I'm telling you this story, my love? Because like my cousin André I'm less troubled by my destiny than by this absurd hope I'm harbouring. Write and tell me what you have decided. Condemn me to winter, or rescue me from it.

Your

Fradique

P.S. The sailors pulled André back inside, untied him, and he resumed command of the boat. Nobody was punished.

Letter to Ana Olímpia
Paris, January 1873

My love,

As I read your letter it sounded so like something I could
have written myself, years ago, when I was young and
thought I knew everything about the passions of the soul.
You write 'Our love was born in secret and as far as I can
see it would have to remain so, slowly breeding shadows
and bitterness – the mould which grows on feelings –
until finally it rots away altogether.' I believe, though,
that there are some feelings more easily corrupted when
exposed to the public light on the squares and the streets.

Holy reliquaries are kept secretly in churches so that
their mystery will preserve them and add to their value.
The most valuable jewels are kept in safes. Holy wisdom
is the exclusive domain of priests, and it is only this
which makes it holy. Any kind of revelation is a kind of
profanation. If our love is sacred, and it is, then it *should*
remain secret.

I have no answer to your second question.

Don't feel sorry for me, condemned to live in winter –
I have brought the memory of the sun with me.

I love you, I must love you always.
Fradique

Letter to Ana Olímpia
Lisbon, July 1876

My treasured friend,

This morning I received a letter from old Arcénio de Carpo setting out the horrible situation you've found yourself in. Unfortunately the letter was delayed in reaching me, as Smith first sent it on to Coimbra where I'd spent some days tracing old roots and renewing old acquaintances; when it arrived I had already left, and the postal service returned it to its sender. So I don't know where you are, or how you are, but if you read this letter I'm sending through young Arcénio it means that something may yet be done.

I set off for Luanda in two weeks, and am going prepared for anything. I needn't ask you to have courage – I know you have it to spare.

Your
Fradique

Letter to Madame de Jouarre
Lisbon, August 1876

My dear godmother,

I'm setting off tomorrow for Angola, rather suddenly and in secret, or at least as much in secret as it is possible for someone to set off for Africa. I'm being driven there by a sad piece of news, so senseless as to be almost unbelievable, and which fills me at once with rage and shame: Ana Olímpia, my dear friend from Angola of whom I've spoken to you so much, has been given over as a slave to some adventurer straight off the boat from Brazil!

As I think you know, Ana Olímpia was born (the daughter of a slave) into the household of a Bahian businessman, Victorino Vaz de Caminha, with whom she came to be married; Victorino did not bother to fill out her freedom papers – obviously because he didn't think it necessary – and he died without this ever having been done. But alas, about six months ago a brother of the dead man turned up in Luanda – one Jesuíno – by all accounts an arrogant, violent man, who for some time had disappeared in pursuit of gold and diamonds within the bounds of Mato Grosso, Bolivia and Paraguay. During the fifty years he spent living in Angola Victorino did not have any contact with him, and even went so far as to tell me that he didn't have any family. Only later he spoke to me of his brother, vaguely, coldly, as though speaking of a stranger. I was left with the impression that some irreparable tragedy had occurred between them.

Jesuíno disembarked in Luanda without warning, accompanied by five black slaves and an Indian servant, and within a short time ran into debts in his sister-in-law's name. He tried to persuade her to lend him the money to build an ice-factory in town, and when this failed he took to discrediting her in public. Finally someone remembered that Victorino had not granted Ana Olímpia her freedom, and that as such she was still a slave, and consequently the property of his next of kin, together with the other slaves, estates, income and machinery the businessman had left. Not even a generous decree from the Marquis de Sá da Bandeira, who eight years ago declared the abolition of slavery in all the colonies and the transition of all slaves to freedom, has been able to help Ana Olímpia, the court considering that precisely because she is a freed slave (!) she ought gratefully to offer her master six years of her service, only then becoming a free woman.

I don't know much more than this, except that my friend is still in Luanda, or at least she was there two months ago, apparently imprisoned in her own house. I am going with no definite plan, more driven by disgust than by reason, but in any case with the firm intention of putting a bullet in this scoundrel (and I don't mean that metaphorically).

I will send news as soon as I arrive.

Your
Fradique

ANGOLA

Letter to Madame de Jouarre
Luanda, September 1876

My dear godmother,

I arrived in Luanda yesterday, on an English clipper. Young Arcénio met me at the docks and told me all the news at once, one piece good and one bad. The good news: Ana Olímpia is still in Luanda; the bad: Jesuíno has sold her (or at least rented her) to Gabriela Santamarinha!

We went to the family mansion in the upper town, where we were met at the door by old Arcénio de Carpo. He embraced me, obviously moved, and as he did so I felt as though I held in my arms a being quite without substance, volatile, the trembling body of a bird. He took me to the library and I noticed that he had been cleaning a rifle. He showed me an impressive collection of weapons: 'Choose one for yourself,' he said to me. 'We're going to war.' He sat on the couch with the shotgun between his knees:

'Victorino Vaz de Caminha was my friend, a great friend; I walked the length of Angola with him, from Quissembo to Bailundo (you can't imagine how big this country is). Now I am near death; I turned eighty-four recently and I feel like a sick old man, I feel as though he and I will be together again someday soon. And when that time comes he will ask me about the wife and the lands he left behind. And what should I say?'

He paused.

'What should I say? Should I tell him that a bandit turned up here, stole his fortune, sold his wife as a slave to a madwoman, and that I just sat by quietly and watched?'

He had tears in his eyes. Later he was to tell me that Jesuíno was about to sell Ana Olímpia's manor to a German company, and had been buying favours with the money he had made, and that before long he would have more influence with the government than Arcénio himself had after half a century living in Angola.

As one of the few Portuguese businessmen to oppose Jesuíno's intentions, old Arcénio is now the main target of the adventurer's wrath: 'That animal has started a sordid campaign against me – he wants to see me in gaol! He's telling everybody that I should be exiled to São Tomé island!' There's no doubt that Arcénio de Carpo should indeed have been arrested and exiled many times before now. There was a governor who tried to do it, but at the time the Colonel was the wealthiest man in Luanda, and the only person who found himself obliged to flee the country was the governor himself, escorted by a battalion of *empacaceiros* (a body of native soldiers; they dress in a doe-skin and belt, and a feathered head-dress, and are armed with nothing but old fowling-pieces) and stoned all his way down to the quayside by the enraged masses. Today Arcénio's money is only enough to allow him to keep up appearances, and I imagine it would not be hard to have him put behind bars.

When I disembarked in Luanda I realized that on the journey I had spent all my hatred for Jesuíno (whom as it happens I don't know personally), and no longer have even the patience to kill him. All I want is simply to free Ana Olímpia, to take her out of here, to take her somewhere she can forget the horror of these terrible days.

But Arcénio thinks differently: 'I have to kill him with my own hands.' He spends his evenings imagining tortures: 'We could roast him on the grill,' he said to me, '*à la mode de* Saint Lawrence'. I reminded him of other equally original deaths – of Admiral Drake, eaten by crabs, of Diomedes, one of Homer's heroes, devoured by his horses; or of Ésquilo, who died after being struck on the top of his bald head by a turtle. He considered a moment: 'That crab one isn't bad. But it would be easier to throw him to the hippos or the alligators.' So he put together a villainous (and cowardly) plan: 'On Saturday,' he said, 'the governor is proposing an alligator hunt on the Bengo River. There are a lot of people going, the creature will be among them, and of course so will we. In that sort of hunt, which can last four or five days, a lot can happen; hunters can get themselves killed by stray bullets. We might be lucky.'

Annoyed, I replied that I thought it a stupid idea, in fact so naïve and so stupid that it might even work, but that I would have no part of it. The Colonel was insistent: 'I have to kill him; and it has to be before I die myself, since afterwards it's likely to be somewhat harder.' I finally agreed to go with him – at least by going with him I might be able to prevent him from doing something foolish.

As for Ana Olímpia, young Arcénio tells me that nothing has been heard of her for several weeks. Gabriela Santamarinha keeps her shut up in the house, which worries me, as the strange lady has lately shown signs of a violent imagination, and the latest word is that she has gone mad. Last year she returned from a drawn-out trip to Brazil with a court of white slavegirls for her household, and soon afterwards organized a huge ball in her house, where she received her guests seated – following the example of the famous Queen Ginga, or Nzinga Mbandi – on the back of one of these slaves. Doubtless they just laughed at her in Brazil, but in Luanda, where the Europeans live in a constant fear of a Negro rebellion, her audacity was seen as a bad omen.

I've thought of going to see her, of asking her directly about Ana Olímpia. It even occurred to me – you can see what I have come to! – to offer her a price for my friend's freedom. But – thank God – I have been able to maintain some prudence and discretion, and although I feel rather as though I'm boiling on a low flame I think that externally I'm still the same serious, distant gentleman who passed through here some years ago – a *touriste* in a white linen suit, in search of intensity and exoticism.

A thousand *saudades*, from your godson,
Fradique

Letter to Madame de Jouarre
Novo Redondo, October 1876

My dear godmother,

Not forty days have gone by since last I wrote to you, but in my life months have passed. It all began with the famous alligator hunt. We set off early one morning, still dark, in light rain; what with all the hunters, slaves and servants, there were some hundred and fifty of us, all divided into two pilot-boats. Having arrived at the Bengo falls we set off towards the inlands in smaller craft, and made our way up the dangerous river, whose strong current drags with it submerged tree-trunks, and forms waves and whirlpools which only the most experienced sailors are able to avoid. 'Abuabuabu' sang the rowers (all native of Cabinda) as they rowed. 'Who turned the world over?' one of them asked in a resonant bass. 'Maria Segunda' the others replied, then repeated the chorus: 'abuabuabu-aiuê-mamauê'. This song continued endlessly, hypnotically, until at last we made land, and it had such an impact on me that now, whenever I have to make some great effort, I catch myself warbling away 'abuabuabu / Who turned the world over? / Maria Segunda / abuabuabu-aiuê-mamauê'.

Having reached the left bank, which is less marshy, we completed the journey on foot and by litter, until we found a large hut which is often used as base-camp for excursions of this kind. Arcénio de Carpo wouldn't lie in a litter to be carried, and insisted on accompanying me on foot, carrying his own gun himself, as if he were not carrying with him the weight of eighty well-lived years but instead perhaps a little over twenty. One of the hunters, teasing him, asked him what he ate to keep himself so tough. Arcénio replied with a shout:

'Hatred!'

The man who was the cause of that hatred was waiting for us, sitting in the shade, a cigar clenched between his

teeth. I recognized him immediately, with the same burning look, the long face, the wild beard that Victorino Vaz
de Caminha had had. Standing to his right, quite oblivious
to the curiosity of the black men and the scorn of the
whites, was a short man, very tanned, with a sharp face,
straight hair held in a ponytail, his body covered with a
woollen poncho. As we approached Jesuíno rose, looked
the Colonel straight in the eye, spat to one side and turned
his back on us to make his way into the hut. I grabbed
Arcénio by the arm in time to stop him from raising his
rifle, but not before the Indian was able to realize what the
old man had meant to do (– this detail is important).

We ate there. It was after one in the afternoon and the
sun shone in all its splendour. Dazed by the excess of
light and the afternoon languor – at that time of day it
almost feels as though life stops still under Africa's skies
– I lay down in a hammock and fell asleep. Arcénio awoke
me before long. He had drunk several cups of *quimbombo*,
a kind of native beer, and his hands were shaking: 'Come
on!' he said. 'The animal is awaiting us in the trap.' Most
of our companions had already gone down towards the
river, sitting in light bamboo canoes, whose sturdiness is
belied by their delicate appearance; I boarded one, with
Arcénio, two servants and four rowers.

That stretch of river runs through dense forest. Its
waters, blocked by the tangled vegetation from the banks
and what I take to be a shady underwater forest, are
full of life. The oars kept becoming enmeshed in the
vegetation and it was necessary to remain attentive to the
movement of the waters, so although the current was
weak our canoe made only slow progress. Occasionally at
one of the bends in the river we would catch sight of one
or other of the vessels, only to lose it again at the next
curve, or behind some islet totally covered in tall grasses.
In none of these boats did we see Jesuíno.

Nor did we see any alligators. 'Do you know the difference between Jesuíno and an alligator?' the Colonel asked me. I said no, I didn't. 'That's his hard luck!' he replied, laughing; 'me neither!' But just the same we continued until dusk fell, without seeing Jesuíno, and as for the alligators the only one we spotted was crucified on a post, in the style of a baroque Christ, in front of a strange hut made of woven reeds and raised up on poles.

It was already night-time when we returned, exhausted, carrying just as many rounds of ammunition as we'd left with. There were blacks and whites dancing around a bonfire, next to which they had strung up the dead animals, just twelve of them, hardly an impressive number if you know that last year an identical group killed fifty-four in a single afternoon.

For dinner they roasted *cacussos*, a very tasty sort of fresh-water fish, abundant in these parts of Africa, and we drank Portuguese wine, *quissangua* and *quimbombo*, the hunters gathering back into groups around the fires. I chatted a bit, enjoying hearing the story of one of the guides – who swore that he had lived as a slave in Guyana for five years, and had come back stowed away on a steamer – until the air was filled with fierce clouds of mosquitoes. Usually these terrible insects would have been kept away by the cigarette smoke and the glow of the bonfires; but there the mosquitoes are insatiable and in my opinion far more dangerous than the alligators. Fearful lest I be eaten alive – and I wasn't far from it – I went inside and (equipped with my mosquito net) set up my hammock by one of the windows where I could at least enjoy the cool night breezes. I remembered a German friend, a great traveller, who some years ago visited Alto Xingu in the Brazilian Amazon: 'When I awoke,' he said, describing it to me, 'I had been so badly bitten by mosquitoes and the itching tormented me so terribly, that I'd started wishing I was a fish so that some cook might scale me.'

Arcénio de Carpo came in not long afterwards, tripping over his own feet and railing at God in Quimbundu and Portuguese, but when I got up to help him he pushed me away rudely: 'Your Excellency may be aware that I am drunk, but I'm not dead yet. And as long as I am alive no man shall ever need to put me to bed.'

It must have been about five in the morning when I woke up, with a green pigeon settled on the netting above my head and a ray of sunshine dancing across my face. I turned my eyes towards the inside of the hut and found it full of people lying in hammocks and on mats, everything in disorder, as if it had been the site of a battle or a bacchanal. Only then did I notice Arcénio de Carpo, lying on his back a couple of metres away from me, very pale and very rigid, and for some reason the image of that crucified alligator came back to me. Becoming alarmed, I got up and shook him, but he didn't move, he stayed quite still, lying straight and solemn, as if someone had nailed him down to the floor.

And they had.

They had driven a long, thin dagger through the middle of his chest, so violently that the blade had gone through his body and the mat and lodged firmly in the hard earth.

The return journey was turbulent and confusing. The days that followed were worse still. Young Arcénio, who had remained in Luanda with business to conduct, heard of his father's death long before our arrival. Even before the pilot-boat had dropped anchor I saw him on the beach, standing at the head of a procession of slaves, a pistol at his waist, a broad-brimmed hat fallen over his face. While the women grieved, crying, shouting, their bodies shaking, the young man silently embraced the body of his father.

He didn't open his mouth till the following morning, after the funeral, to tell me, his voice dark, to prepare my bags, as we might have to leave Angola at any moment. That night at dinner he also told me that he had managed to speak to Ana Olímpia, that she was well and had sent me her good wishes. I said I wanted to see her myself. Arcénio turned to me, and I thought him suddenly old and worn out, but at the same time resolved, sure of himself, with the same unshakable insolence with which his father had gone through his life. 'You will see her,' he said to me, 'we are going to get her out of there.'

That was a Saturday. On the Monday a young lad awoke me in the middle of the night, a candle in his hand, to tell me that Arcénio was waiting for me in the library. I found him dressed in a Colonel's uniform which must have been his father's, and surrounded by the most trustworthy of his men and a few friends. At that moment a female figure emerged from the shadows and embraced me. It was Ana Olímpia.

There was no time to ask questions. 'Let's go!' Arcénio shouted, 'I've got horses waiting and a ship ready to leave from Novo Redondo.' Noticing my astonishment, he shrugged his shoulders: 'I didn't tell you, your Excellency, as you would have prevented me from doing what had to be done – I've killed the animal!'

We left Luanda bathed in spectacular moonlight, galloped across the native quarter of Ingombota, startling dogs awake, knocking down goats, pigs and chickens, thundering over the warm ash of the bonfires, and not until we were in the heart of the bush did we slow the pace and Arcénio de Carpo finally agreed to tell us what had happened. 'I knocked on the animal's door, at two in the morning, and while five of my men overpowered the servants, with no great difficulty as most of them were asleep, I dragged him out of bed and challenged him to a pistol duel.'

Jesuíno had no choice. They went out on to the patio
and as they went he confessed that it had been he who
had given the order to one of his servants – the
Paraguayan – to kill the Colonel. He said that he was glad
to have done it; he said that the father was dead and now
he was going to kill the son. They took their places back
to back, counted ten paces and turned; Arcénio shot first
but missed. He steadied his forearm in his left hand and
aimed, trying to think only of his father and the hatred
bequeathed him through his death. He heard a bitter
laugh, the buzz of the bullet, heard the other man curse
at him in Spanish. Then he fired again and Jesuíno fell
clutching his chest.

I wanted to know what had happened to the Indian.
The young man turned to face me over his shoulder, his
round birds' eyes shining more than ever: 'He ran away!
But your Excellency can be quite sure that I must find
him, even if like Dante I have to go down to hell with a
lamp in my hand!' (Arcénio had never read the classics.)

Freeing Ana Olímpia, he later explained, had been easy:
'I sent another five men to Gabriela Santamarinha's
house. They knocked down the door, tied the poor lady to
her bed, bound the other slaves and left. It may be two or
three days before anybody finds them.'

I did not manage to speak to Ana Olímpia until late in
the morning, when the horses, tortured by the heat and
exhausted by the long journey, had begun to falter. Ahead
of us was a vast sea of arid grasses, lit from the east by a
copper-coloured light, broken up here and there by the
ballerina's silhouette of an acacia tree. We stopped by a
watering-hole and let the animals drink. A massive
baobab tree rose out of the middle of the dark water, huge
and melancholy like a grounded ship. Ana Olímpia
wouldn't speak of what had happened to her over the pre-
ceding months: 'I can't speak about something I don't yet

understand.' Her distant silence, her look of bewilderment, frightened me.

We had lunch right there, five tins of sardines from Nantes, a bit of dried fish roasted on the coals, manioc-flour *funge*, bread and brandy. As we ate Arcénio explained to me the plans for our escape: 'one of my ships set off last night for Cabinda, carrying just the crew, but I put the word about that we were all on it. So nobody knows that we have been travelling by land, and even if they did there is nothing they could do about it – besides they think that we are heading north while we're actually going south. There's a brig waiting for us in Novo Redondo with a cargo of slaves bound for Pernambuco.'

I looked at him, confused. A slaving ship? I told him that I would have nothing to do with it. Arcénio shrugged his shoulders: 'Your Excellency doesn't have much choice in the matter. I myself had no choice. In this matter, nobody does.' We were in the middle of this conversation, Ana Olímpia beside us, silent and distant, when we saw a group of Quissama people approaching us – men and women, all alike wrapped in cotton cloths, their hair separated laboriously into little braids, with red glass beads on the tips, bodies rubbed with palm oil. Tied to the end of a rope they were dragging a scrawny boy, covered in wounds, a gazelle's startled look in his eyes.

One of the men, whose hair was covered by a spectacular kind of bowler-hat, approached us and pointed at the boy, shouting something I didn't understand. Arcénio laughed: 'He's asking if we want to buy a slave.' I refused, furious, and the boy threw himself at my feet, crying and wailing. 'If we don't buy him, they'll kill him,' Arcénio explained. 'That's what I was going to explain to you. By buying a slave you're saving his life.' In his way of looking at things, Negro-trafficking is like a kind of philanthropy. He loves the Negroes – just as his father did – and that's why he sells them to Brazil. He believes that the days of slavery are numbered over there in Pedro II's great land, and that once they've been freed the wretches will be better off there than they now are here.

At four in the afternoon we set off again, taking the young boy with us, and as night fell we reached Calumbo, on the right bank of the Quanza, where a white man was there to meet us, a friend of Arcénio's who ran a lucrative provisions store nearby. Justino – or Kituto as the natives called him – was an old retired military man, who listened to our explanations for our presence there without saying a word, and even after Arcénio had finished speaking he remained silent. At last he stood up and embraced him.

That night I managed to sleep fairly comfortably, stretched out on an improvised bed between sacks of *cabulo* beans, barrels of Portuguese wine and various batches of exquisitely made bowler-hats. Kituto gave his room up to Ana Olímpia, but when I saw her the next morning I knew that she had spent a sleepless night. 'I can't sleep,' she told me. 'No sooner do I close my eyes than I start seeing all those things I don't want to see.'

We crossed the river on one of the merchant's rafts and the following evening, after another night of sleeping out, made our way into the little town of Novo Redondo – 'Quisala', to use the natives' name for it. The people gathered in the streets, alarmed at our bandit-like appearance, and Arcénio had to use his whip to clear our path through to the house of his uncle, his mother's brother Horácio Benvindo, a very tall, very dignified, very black man who came to meet us riding on a camel. His companion Lívia, a magnificent woman with soft golden hair, was the grand-daughter of a Neapolitan merchant, Nicolau Tabana, who had come here to raise a fortune and a family. Tabana had come to Novo Redondo in 1818 with another twenty-four Italians, all exiled (I was never able to find out whether their crime was a political one or not), which explains the large number of mulattos and *cabritos* (the name they now give to the children of white men with half-caste women) you find in this area. Horácio Benvindo's house, one of the few in the town to have been built in the European style, was all dressed up to receive us. The fair Lívia, smiling in the doorway as we approached, looked like an angel at the gates to heaven.

Ana Olímpia, who for three nights hadn't slept, dismounted trembling and hesitant, took five steps as if in a sort of slow dance, and collapsed senseless into my arms. I took her inside, to the little room Lívia had appointed for her, and lay her out on the bed. Two days have now passed, and – feverish and delirious – she lies there still. Lívia, who has inherited from her father a strange gift for herbal remedies, has treated her devotedly, but it seems that none of her brews, her scents or ointments has so far had any effect. I thought of calling Luís Gonzaga in Benguela, the only doctor for many miles. Arcénio disillusioned me; it would take him a good five days to reach us, perhaps a week, and we will have to be back on our way sooner than that.

This letter will go off to Luanda tomorrow, with a *pombeiro* who works for Horácio Benvindo. By the time you receive it I will probably already be in Brazil. I have friends in Pernambuco and in São Salvador de Bahia, and although they aren't expecting me they will I hope give us a warm welcome. But could you please ask the invaluable Smith to transfer 20,000 francs in my name to the Bank of Brazil?

Arcénio de Carpo's brig is called the *Nação Crioula*, the 'Creole Nation'. In an attempt to offer me some kind of consolation he has said that the *Nação Crioula* might well be the very last slaving ship in history. Travelling on the last slaving ship strikes me as a strange honour, but he is quite right – truly we have no choice.

Your loving godson,
Fradique

BRAZIL

Letter to Madame de Jouarre
Olinda, December 1876

My dear godmother,

Dusk seems to have crept up on me rather suddenly as I've been getting ready to write this, sitting at a stone table in the gardens of the beautiful colonial palace where we're all now staying (owned by none other than Arcénio de Carpo). The evenings never seem to last here, they end abruptly, violently, in a broad blaze that quickly burns itself out into grey and melancholy. But unlike in western Africa, unlike what somehow I still always expect to happen, the sun doesn't sink into the sea; rather the water darkens, turning almost black, and the darkness seems to rise out from it.

I imagine that you must by now have received the letter I sent you from Novo Redondo, and so you must know why I'm here. From my seat at this table I can see the city, the houses all painted in wild colours, the colonial mansions, the baroque churches and tall palm trees, and they lie over the hills rolling out towards the vast darkness. Novo Redondo is on the other side of that darkness, twenty-five days away by boat, three and a half thousand miles, almost at the same parallel chosen by the Portuguese nobleman Duarte Coelho Pereira when he gave his orders for Olinda to be built three centuries ago.

Our last night in Novo Redondo was spent in a contin-
uous party, a peculiar spectacle organized in our honour
by Horácio Benvindo which lasted until nightfall on the
following day, when under cover of dark the *Nação Crioula*
raised anchor and pulled away from the dock. I had
decided to take Ana Olímpia with us. Although I was
unsure about how well she was, I nonetheless thought it
better to risk the crossing, knowing that I could get her
better treatment in Pernambuco, than to leave her there
in that middle-of-nowhere and trust her to the question-
able inspiration of a blonde sorceress. But as soon as the
rumblings of the first fireworks could be heard, my friend
awoke with a start, as if being drawn back suddenly from
another life, and she soon got out of bed to watch the
euphoria of the people outside.

Horácio Benvindo had had a large table set up in the
church square, with trays of roast meat (*pacassa*, wild pig
and birds of all kinds), three barrels of good Madeira wine
and others of rum, and after a long speech (during which
he recited a sonnet of his own in memory of old Arcénio
de Carpo) he invited the whole village to drink with us.
Then a band took to the stage, eight musicians, five of
them blowing incredible ivory cornetts, the other three
beating different kinds of drums. The cornetts, made
from elephant tusks and decorated with geometrical
shapes in black, red and yellow paint, were each more
than a metre long and produced a very loud, hoarse
sound, like the roaring of some prehistoric beast.

It didn't take long for the band's wild rhythms to take
hold of the crowd. Horácio and Lívia soon fell to dancing,
and eventually even I did too, to the horror of Arcénio de
Carpo who watched over all the proceedings with uncon-
cealed disdain. It was the kind of rhythm where the
dancers usually form a ring, in the middle of which one of
them develops a series of steps which the others applaud;

after some time this dancer chooses another, approaches them and gives them a nudge with their belly, the *semba*, passing the chosen one into the middle of the circle. I had to dance in the middle of the ring myself, my natural incompetence providing no little entertainment for everybody else, and in particular to Ana Olímpia, who – though she could not join us – watched the party from her place in a wicker chair.

In the middle of the night I saw a small group of men arriving with their hands tied behind their backs. Horácio ordered them to be released and they mingled in with the rest of the crowds, singing and dancing, drinking and eating, as if unaware of their destiny, or as if in that way they might be able to forget it. It wasn't until the early hours that they were grouped back together and herded on to the boat. The captain of the *Nação Crioula*, a sombre man with very blue eyes and a thick red beard, who I later learned was a native of Ílhavo, pointed at the group, saying to me, 'In each of them I can see a hectare of land I'm going to buy in southern Brazil. What with the end of the trade, nowadays thirty slaves are worth as much as three hundred were worth twenty years ago.'

Horácio Benvindo looked at him with loathing:

'Maybe they'll hang you before that,' he muttered. 'Maybe the English will catch you and hang you.'

The captain returned the glare. 'I suppose it would be only fair. It's a day I've been awaiting for twenty years.'

Lívia appeared suddenly with a tray laden with roasted grasshoppers. 'Try one,' she said, turning towards me and the captain: 'they're lovely'. And they were indeed very good, with the slight pungency of hazelnut and the consistency of little shrimps. The captain described how he had once – after a great storm – spent a week adrift right on the Equator, in that hot, desolate region which sailors call 'the snare', like a sea of oil, quite dead, with no breeze to swell their sails. All their provisions had been lost, and the sailors were already talking about killing some of the slaves to eat them, when all of a sudden they saw the sky turn dark above them and a vast cloud of grasshoppers dropped down on to the water. 'Over the next three weeks we ate nothing but grasshoppers, roasted, stewed, fried and sautéed; and not only did we not have to lose a single slave but when we arrived they were all fat and glowing, and were able to fetch us a very good price!'

Do you find Angolan cuisine revolting? Don't forget that among the Roman aristocracy grasshoppers – lovingly roasted in honey – were a great delicacy. In fact, the Romans were particularly enthusiastic insect-eaters. At rich men's tables you could find, for instance, beetle larvae seasoned in wine and grilled. In ancient Greece they would use infusions of various bugs to treat persistent fevers, and even today in some countries in Central Europe exactly the same is done with a tea made from the common domestic cockroach. Back in my own country, in my very own Lisbon, we go to cheap taverns to eat little snails, cooked in water, salt and oregano, which are a snack much enjoyed by the masses.

My final image of Angola, which I can see again now, quite clearly, is of Horácio Benvindo, sitting on his camel and followed by a boisterous crowd, all of them lit up by the dazzling light of the bonfires on the beach. From where we stood that night, far out on the deck of the *Nação Crioula*, the bonfires became blurred in with the stars. 'When I was a child I'd often watch the departure of the slaves, and always wondered how they felt,' said Ana Olímpia. 'Now I know.'

In the hold the slaves were singing. The captain had ordered a big cage to be left on deck, filled with chickens, pheasants and little song-birds, and the noises of the forest mingled with the sad lament of the Negroes, with a strange effect on my mood. The ship opened up the waters ahead of it, while behind us it left just a thread of light, what I think is called the *ardenthya maritima*, which sailors believe to be the souls of the drowned trying to find their way up to heaven.

The captain had given up his usual larger, more comfortable room to Ana Olímpia, so he was crammed into a tiny cabin with me and Arcénio de Carpo. On that first night I discovered that it was impossible to get to sleep there; even if I opened the little hatch the heat was so intense that I was barely able to breathe. So I followed the example of the sailors, all of them Brazilians, black or half-caste, and hung my hammock out on the deck, and I fell asleep beneath the stars.

At the end of the second day I asked the captain to allow the slaves to come up on deck, in groups of five, just to get some sun and some exercise, to which he agreed. Ana Olímpia managed to understand something of their tongue, similar to the beautiful and resonant language of the Congolese (whose words seem to be made up entirely of vowels), helped as well by the fact that many already spoke some elementary Portuguese. There were thirty of them. Most had lost their freedom for minor crimes, for theft or adultery, others because of some mysterious conspiracy, for practising witchcraft or on some other equally absurd charge.

One of them, whom we called the Count of Cagliostro, or just The Count, a tall, strong man with a severe expression, had managed to bring with him a fetish, a doll carved out of red wood, which he used whenever he had a decision to make, or when he wanted news of those he had left behind. He would begin by venerating the little idol, praising its beauty and its gifts, enumerating one by one all the wonders of which it was capable, and finally he would ask it his question. After each question he would bring the doll up to his ear and sit silently, while it gave him its clear responses to his most intimate worries, or told him, word for word, the latest *maka* (that is, dispute) to take place between the elders of his village. Another slave wanted news of his mother whom he had left sick, or of his wife whose fidelity he doubted, and to all these questions the little idol would – always through the Count as its intermediary – give its helpful answer.

One evening Arcénio de Carpo (meaning to ridicule the man) asked after his mother, Joana Benvindo, whom he had left in the capital in a state of great anxiety. The Count was not in the least bit put out. He asked his doll the question, going through the whole usual ritual, then spent a moment listening. 'The old lady is drinking to your death,' he said. 'She is eating to your death.' By this he meant that Joana Benvindo, believing her son dead, was performing his comba-ri-toquê, the ceremony in which the living celebrate the dead, drinking and eating in their honour. This revelation didn't please Arcénio de Carpo at all: 'Nonsense!' he snarled. 'The real Count of Cagliostro would have done better.'

When they want to ask the fetish a question, the Negroes get a hammer and hammer a nail into it. If the question is answered the nail will be removed, and the statue fêted and given aquavitae. If not the nail will stay, eaten away by rust, to remind the little idol of its incompetence and punish him for it. On this matter the captain remembered how here in Brazil the images of our numerous little Catholic saints are often made to seem human – and so they are treated as humans too. According to him, one evening when he had gone to visit an important plantation owner, he saw this man violently flogging a life-sized statue of Saint Anthony whom he held responsible for the flight of his best slave: 'Is this how you look after my slaves?! I'll teach you a lesson, you vagabond,

you crook, you friend to the Negroes!' The captain
assures me that there are even special whips, which come
in various sizes, made especially to punish saints who are
particularly indolent.

Personally I was impressed by the Count and his
extraordinary doll. If it is possible (as I'm told it is) to
transmit the human voice great distances along simple
copper wires, then who is to say that a doll shouldn't be
able to have visions and the power of speech? Just imagine, my dear godmother, if it were to become common for
you and me to use talking idols! I can see you in your
winter garden, in the cool half-light between the rose-
bushes, getting hold of a crude fetish, gaily asking it for
news of our dear Bertrand (and where is Bertrand?), a tip
for the races or just a precise weather forecast.

On our long journey I was also struck by an episode
that I must tell you about: one night one of the crew, a
young man with a warm voice, accompanied on the
guitar, began to sing a sad *moda* in which I thought (surprised) that I recognized some lines of Castro Alves:

> *'Lord God of the wretched!*
> *Tell me, my Lord God,*
> *If I rave . . . or if it's true*
> *There's such horror beneath heaven?! . . .*

> *Oh, sea, why won't you wash away*
> *With the sponges of your waves*
> *This foul blot upon your cloak?*

> *Stars! Nights! Storms!*
> *Turn over the immensities!*
> *Typhoon, sweep away the seas!'*

It comes from the great Bahian poet's 'Slaving Ship'.

> *'My God, my God! What flag is that*
> *That on the topsail dances boldly?'*

the young sailor's song asked, his dark face illuminated
by the gentle light from the moon.

> *'Cry, my Muse, oh cry so hard*
> *That the banner is washed in your tears! . . .*
> *Banner of my land, green and golden*
> *That Brazil's breeze kisses and sways,*
> *Standard that draws in the sunlight,*
> *You who from liberty after the war*
> *Were raised by the heroes, up on their lances;*
> *Better they tear you on the battlefield,*
> *Than you ever serve your people as a shroud!'*

I approached, confused and moved, and asked where
he had learnt those lines. 'It's only a song, sir' the young
man replied. I argued that it wasn't just any song, that the
words had been written by one of Brazil's greatest poets
in protest against the slave trade. The sailor looked at me
doubtfully. 'It's just a song,' he insisted. 'I know nothing
of politics.'

We entered Brazilian waters just as twenty-four days
earlier we had left Africa's, silent and invisible, under
cover of darkness on a moonless night. The slaves who
had crossed the Atlantic over these past years, enclosed in
filthy cellars for twenty or thirty days, must all have
stepped out on to the same beach as I did; blind and confused, they must have felt sure that they had been
through a single endless night on the seas.

A flimsy *falua*, a sort of barge with a very tall lateen sail,
led us to the beach, floating on the warm water lightly
and calmly as if it were levitating. I wanted to know the
name of the region: 'Porto das Galinhas', the captain told
me. 'It's paradise.' It had been called 'Porto das Galinhas',
the port of the chickens, because every time a ship docked
there to unload slaves, the word would spread through
the bush, among the farmers – a secret signal: 'there are

chickens in the port'. The thirty men who had been brought over with us on the *Nação Crioula* were taken to a nearby house, almost hidden among the tall palms, where they were washed and dressed. They were sold that very morning (for a good price, as I was later told), and taken at once on foot to various farms in the south of the country. Arcénio would not let me watch the deal being struck. 'The less Your Excellency knows, the less we need trouble your clear conscience.'

We continued our own journey on horseback, to the city of Pernambuco, a hundred kilometres or so towards the north. Ana Olímpia, who had again become distant and silent, almost a sleep-walker, didn't say a word during the whole journey. But when dusk began to fall and the first lights of the city began to rise up ahead of us she turned to me, her large eyes brimming with tears: 'Why did you come with me?' What answer could I give her? I said nothing. If one day someone sets out to write my biography they will find nothing but silences.

Arcénio de Carpo has a colonial mansion in the city of Olinda, which his father bought many years ago when he was first thinking about leaving Angola. And it is here that we are lodged, recovering from the emotions and struggles of the last few months and trying to recover the thread of our lives. As I write night has already fallen. I can hear Ana Olímpia, walking in the garden, singing a simple little *moda* I often heard in Luanda from the thumb-piano-players and the old grocery-women. She has an amazing voice, charged with shadows yet at the same time clear and warm as if it were made of liquid light. It is the first time I have heard her sing since we arrived in Brazil.

What am I doing here?

A thousand *saudades*, from your godson,
Fradique

Letter to Madame de Jouarre
Olinda, February 1877

My dear godmother,

I'm writing with some rather morbid news: I've died! If you are to believe a letter that arrived yesterday from Joana Benvindo in Luanda, we've all died – Ana Olímpia, Arcénio de Carpo and I; it happened when our pilot-boat was shipwrecked, somewhere between Ambriz and Quissembo. Did I tell you that Arcénio sent one of his ships to set out towards Cabinda on the night of our flight in an attempt to confuse anyone who might try to follow us? Pursued by a Portuguese sloop Arcénio's pilot-boat came too close to the coast as its crew tried to disembark, and ended up being hurled by the waves against a rocky reef. So Joana Benvindo decided to mourn the death of her son, even though he was known to be alive, and she wept for his death so magnificently and authentically, with banquets and drumming, that at last his body even showed up, somewhat gnawed on by the fish, and was buried in the cemetery at Alto das Cruzes.

The *Comércio de Angola*, a newspaper belonging to an old friend of the Colonel's, announced the news of the tragedy, lamenting the death of one of the most respected children-of-the-country, 'who was, like his father, the victim of a rootless bandit, a man with neither honour nor decency, who seems to have landed in Angola on an errand from the Devil with the sole aim of sowing trouble and discord, mourning and terror'. The article allowed two lines of adjectives for me, which doubtless were intended as compliments even though in the mouth of men like Father Nicolau dos Anjos they were terrible insults: 'the bard of modernity', 'the prophet of naturalism', 'a Demonic poet', 'a restless adventurer', etc.

And another piece of bad news: Jesuíno is alive! The *Comércio de Angola* described how the brigand was discovered by two policemen in the small hours, unconscious and bleeding heavily, but that the doctor who saw him had confirmed that the bullet hadn't hit any vital organ, and two weeks later he was already out and about in the town, boasting of his luck and mocking ours. To my surprise this miracle didn't displease Arcénio: 'So much the better,' he said. 'It's as it is so that I can kill him again.' Ideally he would like to kill Jesuíno a thousand times, and each time revive him to kill him again: a gunshot, a stabbing, beating him to death with sticks or punches, by impaling him, poisoning him with curare, strangling him, hanging him, tying him to a stake and burning him, crucifying him to a baobab tree in the sun, throwing him over a cliff, drowning him, bleeding him to death, crushing him in a pit filled with plaster, guillotining him – in brief, killing him in as many imaginative and cruel ways as man has ever killed since humanity made its first appearance on this planet.

The good news is that besides your letter I've also received the 20,000 francs (with recriminations from my faithful Smith), and can now make plans for the future a little more calmly. I now spend my time wandering around Olinda and Pernambuco, cities so close to each other that in truth the first is really just a district of the second. Pernambuco covers two islands, which the Capibaribe, Beberibe and Pina rivers separate from the continent. In its streets you can smell the same melancholy which surprised me in Luanda, a lethargy which is transmitted from the people to their homes, as if the whole population had already died and their city fallen into ruin. And yet there are some wealthy districts here too. The rich are loathsomely rich, and all the more rich and loathsome for the contrast with the extreme

wretchedness of the people. In Santo Antonio the mansions hide luxuriant gardens, which at night form the
settings for romantic dances, while the Negroes sleep,
exhausted, in their straw hovels.

Ana Olímpia and I went to one of these dances at the
house of Alexandre Gomes, a childhood friend of mine
from back home, who has set up a cigar factory in this city.
His wife Isabel, the only daughter of the Baron of Itaparica,
lived in Lisbon for some time, where her greatest pride was
to have caught a glimpse – one night at the opera – of the
melancholy profile of Feliciano de Castilho. Apart for this
insistence on admiring the poet of 'The Castle Night',
Isabel is a happy, clever woman with a dangerous wit and
an equally refined critical spirit. We were dancing a gay
mazurka when I looked up and noticed the extraordinary
pallor of the man playing the piano, and wondered whether
the poor man had suffered a fainting-fit.

'Is he dead?' I asked Isabel.

'Oh yes, he died, going on for five years ago.'

Apparently the pianist had arrived in Brazil from Paris
accompanied by his wife Chantal, a young dancer whose
blonde, careless beauty still divides the opinions of Per-
nambucanos into two warring factions: women are on
one side, the cruder sex (to which I belong) on the other.
Within a few months Chantal had attracted around her a
noisy swarm of admirers, most notable among whom was
a still-young doctor who had studied in Paris where
(passing his leisure time between *bistro* and *bistro*, *cabaret*
and *cabaret*) he had contracted that incurable disturbance
of the spirit we tend to call 'scepticism'. Within a few
months the whole town was following the illicit relationship with such fervour, kiss by kiss, sigh by sigh, and the
betrayed husband began to receive messages from anonymous informants. One night, as Chantal – radiant in gold
and sequins – was getting ready to go out, the pianist

grabbed her by the arm, threw her against the wall, and killed her with two gunshots to her breast.

At the trial the judge acquitted him, as the letter of the law said he should, and he returned in triumph to Pernambucan society. Triumphant, yes, but now – and forever afterwards – deathly pale: 'Everybody wants to meet him,' Isabel explained. 'He has become a sort of monument, a sort of fashion – no successful party can afford to be without him.' I turned to look at the man again: stiff, his hair loose and very black, with no trace of blood in his face. 'He looks like a vampire', I observed. 'He is a vampire!' Isabel agreed, 'a vampire surrounded by vampires.' She pointed out another man, tall, dark, who was standing at the other end of the room in animated conversation with a group of youths. 'That one's the doctor. He showed great feeling when Chantal died. He even had the girl's remains exhumed secretly, and when word of that got around (which didn't take long) people found his devotion very moving.'

And do you want to know what the tragic lover did next? He had the skeleton cleaned, put together and articulated, and kept it in his wardrobe. And today, during animated salons of 'speculative philosophy', whenever he wants to illustrate to his friends the emptiness of the human condition, he opens the cupboard and takes out Chantal (or at least what's left of her). 'After death,' he says, 'this is what becomes of a most beautiful woman'.

I left the ball, almost dragging Ana Olímpia, leaving the vampires dancing their crazy mazurka in the hall. She was startled: 'Has something happened?' I reassured her. 'No, nothing; I'm just not used to living in this world.' My friend smiled: 'Then let's leave this world for somewhere far away.' I thought of a proposition that Alexandre had just made me, that I travel with him to visit a farm in São Francisco do Conde, a little town in the

depths of Bahia, some 200 kilometres from Salvador.
Alexandre is going there on business – he's considering
buying the farm – but thought the trip might be advan-
tageous for me too, since, as he says: 'It's a chance for
you to study the real, authentic Brazil, the Brazilian
Brazil; you will never understand it here, where it is
ashamed of its nature and tries idiotically to transform
itself into a European country.'

For the first time it occurred to me that I could set
myself up somewhere like that, somewhere far from the
din of the world, watching the earth endlessly giving forth
fruit, accompanied at dusk by the song of the Negroes
around their bonfires, hunting and fishing, drinking fresh
water from the streams, eating black beans and dried
meat, tapioca, the mangoes and bananas from my
orchard. So I decided to accept Alexandre's invitation,
and I leave for Salvador tomorrow. But do write to me, do
keep sending me news of that damned metropolis, the
echoes of all the wars, the rumours and murmurings.
Don't forget the court intrigues, even the most sordid,
the literary feuds, the roarings of the politicians, the
noisy accounts of the latest crimes. And tell me too what
has become of the friends I left there, defeated by life, at
the sad tables of the Café da Paz.

Your
Fradique

Letter to Ana Olímpia
Cajaíba Plantation, March 1877

My love,

They say that in 1815 when Napoleon left the island of Elba and landed with a handful of faithful followers in Cannes, the governor of Lyon sent the following sequence of messages to Paris:

— The Corsican monster has escaped from his cage, but there is no cause for concern. His end is already planned.

— The usurper is heading for Grenoble, but the people do not follow him, the country does not recognize him. He shall soon face his punishment.

— General Bonaparte has entered Grenoble. The people flee ahead of him. There is a power advancing towards the city, a power that must soon expel the tyrant.

— Napoleon is marching to this great city. We will fight him to the death.

— The Emperor entered Lyon, loudly cheered on by the people. May God bless the restoration of the Empire, for on it depends the happiness of France!

Fulfilling my promise to tell you everything – my every step, every thought, every exchange of words – I began on Monday to take notes of things that had been happening to me since we parted at the Cais de Ramos in Pernambuco. And today as I was rereading what I had written I remembered the governor of Lyon.

Monday: 'This landscape has not yet been inaugurated. Everything is new, as if it were the very first day of all. I have given one of the islands your name. Paradise might have been here; and it is certainly here amid these forests that the Lord God now is resting, recovering from that huge disaster that was the creation of mankind.'

Tuesday: 'Awoke very early. Had a cup of bitter coffee and went out for a swim. Spent the evening alone around the village, imagining that I had you here with me, your arm in mine, while the sun set the mountains and the houses aflame. I could live here, with you, until the ending of all the centuries.'

Wednesday: 'All evenings here are always the same evening. The village is like an engraving. Today I climbed the Recôncavo Mountain on foot, and stayed at the top for some time, looking out at the Baía de Todos-os-Santos, the bay with its sleeping islands, its birds circling half-asleep, an amazing sea that never moves. Eternity is not the inexhaustible sum of all the centuries, quite the contrary – it must surely be this absence of time. Absolute calm (which can be more than a little dull!).'

Thursday: 'I already know all the slaves (and there are 150 of them!) by name, their surnames too. Ernesto, the foreman, was born right here at the Cajaíba Plantation. He knows the whole history of the region, everything since the arrival of the Portuguese in 1561, and to hear him speak about it you could almost believe that he had arrived on those first caravels himself, that he had danced and drunk with the Indians, founded the plantations, built the church and the convent.'

Friday: 'Went to see the orchard. Ernesto assured me that if the ripe oranges are not harvested they will go back to being green, that they will stay fresh another year and will be even tastier then. I think this miracle is conclusive proof that the Garden of Eden was indeed situated somewhere around here! This would also explain the other remaining traces of eternal life flourishing among the waters and the trees: drowsiness, silence, the sleeping sea. In truth so much eternity can begin to grow tedious. Alexandre has decided not to buy the farm; should I buy it myself?'

Saturday: 'Dreamt of the restless trampling of throngs of people in the streets of Paris. There is not a soul to be found in this landscape. I fear that if we move here we will soon die of boredom, or – worse – we would live too long, living out lengthy bored-to-death lives. I am sure it would be better not to buy the farm.'

That is what I wrote. Today, Monday, I bought the farm. I bought it for us, in the hope that it will serve us as a good haven until we can find ourselves some better destiny. Have I done well?

I love you,
Fradique

Letter to Eça de Queiroz
Cajaíba Plantation, March 1877

My dear José Maria,

So, do you want to know what this worthy friend of yours has been up to these past months? Prepare yourself for a shock: I've bought a farm! Twenty thousand hectares of fine land in the Bahian Recôncavo, a couple of hundred kilometres from São Salvador, together with all its 150 slaves, a luxurious manor-house, quarters for the slaves (a *sanzala*, or *senzala* as they call it here), an infirmary, a large yard (tiled), two steam-powered engines, a turbine, a machine for making cornmeal and another for crushing cassava, boilers and presses, stills, casks, and other equipment for making sugar. This farm of mine is called Cajaíba, named for the island it's located on, at the mouth of the river Seriji, right opposite the old town of São Francisco do Conde, and used to belong to Field-Marshal Alexandre Gomes de Argolo Ferrão, Baron of Cajaíba. The main house, a broad, beautiful building turned towards the sea and surrounded by tall imperial palms, was built about forty years ago on the ruins of an older manor, which the people of this region believed to be haunted by the spirit of a famous slave-trader.

So I have been transformed into a plantation-owner, one of those men who for centuries have exercised unique authority in these vast backwoods, all the greater and more feared for the fact that I'm sure nobody here has ever seen Emperor Pedro II, nor even a picture of him. To the poor slaves the great landowners are the closest they can imagine to an incarnation of God. They treat us just as one would expect, with a reverential terror (what their masters like to call respect) and a sort of devotion which – when seen closer up – is no more than an odd mixture between loathing and impotence.

The slave revolts which Haiti and Jamaica suffered with for years, which transformed the lives of the French and English settlers into bloody nightmares, have had no equivalent here in Brazil. There have been rebellions, yes, but only in the good old Portuguese style – the occasional skirmish, twenty or so here in Bahia this century, each leading to the stabbing of one farmer or other, and all of which were rapidly quelled. Almost all were led by old Nago warriors, Mohammedans, reduced to slavery by a religious conflict which for years continued to unsettle the Yoruba empire. And why did these warlike men of faith fail? These men with God and strategy on their side, not to mention despair, which we know in these cases to be the strongest ally of all?

If you read the reports of the trials that followed the most recent of these, the 1835 rebellion, you will see why: the Africans had to face not just the strength of the white men but – far worse than this – the mistrust of the blacks born here, the Creole Negroes, for whom Brazil is the only true homeland and for whom a life of slavery is the only life they have ever known.

We have an old Nigerian from the Hausa tribe living here at the Cajaíba Plantation, a universally respected man who took part in the 1835 rebellion. Cornélio (for that is what they call him) claims to be the only survivor of a shipload of 200 slaves brought over in 1828 from the Nigerian coast. He describes how two days after they set sail the slaves began to die of a strange and horrible disease, a sort of devastating leprosy, that in the space of a few hours opened up wounds all over the body, rotted the limbs and drove the men to madness. The first bodies were removed from the hold by the sailors, but one of them then contracted the disease and he too had to be thrown howling into the sea, and from then on the others refused to go down below. Cornélio watched a young woman bite her own son to death, before herself being killed by other slaves; he saw men without faces, men like ghosts, eating rats; he watched the rats themselves ('the rats' he said, 'were enormous, they were practically people. They talked to me.'). He was witnessing Hell and all its demons. When he managed to get out of there (he can't remember how) and realized he was still alive he became convinced that he was immune to death. This conviction made him an extremely dangerous man. He took part in every revolt in Salvador, and was whipped, lashed, tortured, chained up by the neck in a flooded cell, hanged naked and upside-down in the scorching heat of the bushland sun. And he survived it all, finally ending up here at the Cajaíba Plantation where everyone treats him with respect and affection.

Cornélio, as I told you to begin with, was in the 1835 rebellion. He told me that if they had triumphed the rebels had planned to burn all the Catholic images in the Terreiro de Jesus. The white men were to be decapitated and the half-castes and Creoles enslaved and taken to Africa. 'The mulattos and Creole blacks always betrayed us,' he told me. 'But we didn't want to kill them; after all, they are our blood. But they betrayed us that time too. If there had been another revolt not one would have been allowed to live!'

After 1835 no Hausa man was ever sold in Brazil again, which might go some way towards explaining why the rebellions came to an end too. The slaves who have disembarked in Pernambuco and São Salvador in recent years are for the most part natives of Angola, the Congo, Gabon and Mozambique, they are mostly countryfolk with little training in the arts of war, and with no desire whatsoever to start any trouble. The Angolans, who are seen as good workers, can fetch a good price. The opposite is the case with the Negroes from Mozambique, who are considered by people around here to be (in Alexandre's words) 'a poor, ugly race of listless, lazy men who tend towards melancholy,' and command lower prices than slaves from any other nation.

The Gabonais suffer just as acute *saudades* for Africa. Many kill themselves, by refusing food or just eating large quantities of earth. Not so long ago the earth-eaters were even punished by being made to wear grotesque iron masks. The heat from the sun stuck the masks to their faces and caused horrific deformities. This practice has now been abandoned; but this is not because the plantation owners have become more humane, rather because the end of the trade has meant that slaves have become more valuable commodities, and are therefore to be protected.

The women of Costa da Mina, extraordinarily beautiful with their cheerful fabrics, their bracelets of glass beads and muslin head-dresses, have always seemed to me to be more elegant than their mistresses, and are treated like royalty on the streets of Pernambuco and São Salvador. The men from that country, with their distinctive athletic bearing and their natural arrogance that so annoys the Europeans, are mainly used as porters for pianos.

The position of porter is actually the most common among the so-called wage-slaves. They are the men who carry the sedan-chairs, the traded merchandise, the stone for building work. So from north to south – or, as we say here, from Oiapoque to Chui – it is the blacks who are carrying Brazil on their shoulders. Nothing moves in the cities without them, nothing gets done or built, and out in the country nothing is grown without their strength. I've even seen a young gentleman crossing the street to buy a cabbage at the market opposite, and come out a moment later, walking ever so tall and elegant, ever so dignified, followed by a huge Negro with his wicker basket on his head, containing . . . the cabbage!

Many wage-slaves manage to buy their freedom after twenty or twenty-five years. Once free they go right back to carrying merchandise, night and day, till at last they themselves can afford to acquire a slave to do their work for them. The coffee-porters, whose exhausting labour is accompanied by the best rewards, should in theory be able to buy their freedom after just ten years' work. But few live long enough for this, and what money they do manage to accumulate passes straight back into the pockets of their masters.

My farm lies beside São Francisco da Barra do Sergipe do Conde (a rather excessive name for such a small place), founded in 1561 by Portuguese adventurers in search of gold, and which today is barely more than a sleepy little fishing-village. Bit by bit I have come to recognize the friendliness that comes as consolation in this little place, where one celebration justifies another and everywhere visitors are welcomed with open arms. Visitors who call in the morning tend to be offered a glass of liqueur, usually home-made and always excellent, *cachaça*, or a refreshing local drink, *guaraná*, to which the Brazilians attribute all manner of regenerative virtues. In the evening the drink is accompanied by little cakes and coffee. And there is almost always a piano (more's the pity); I've already counted more than fifty! On Sundays the night is filled with tortured chords, and even down the darkest alleys you can hear 'The Monastery Bells' clanging away endlessly.

As for the festivities I mentioned, I was able to be present at an unusual carnival performance, called *cucumbis* here and *congadas* in Pernambuco, which every year brings out large numbers of Negroes dressed in feathers, dancing and singing. The groups, which represent the Congolese court and all its personalities, the King and Queen, princes and princesses, nobles, the Tongue (the interpreter), the magician, fools and sooth-sayers – sing in Portuguese and in a language which must be African in origin, while at the same time they shake rattles, beat adufos, tambourines and agogo-drums, play marimbas and thumb-pianos (here called *quissanges*). The basic costume is made up of long, striking feathers tied at the knees, the waist, the arms and the wrists, rich necklaces with red headbands, goat-hide ankle-boots decorated with ribbons and braids, tight, flesh-coloured trousers and shirts, and around the necks of the men and women strings of teeth and coral. Typically the king is dressed in a rich fine velvet cloak, carries a sceptre and wears a golden crown. At the *cucumbi* that I watched the monarch was a small man with a head as smooth as an egg and a rather helpless expression which contrasted in every way with the hoarse, powerful voice with which he sang and led the group:

> *I'm the King of Congo and I have come to play*
> *I've just arrived from Portugal*

To which his court would reply in chorus:

> *Ê . . . ê . . . sembangalá*
> *I've just arrived from Portugal*

Then the rhythm of the music would change, as would the king's nationality:

> *Viva our Black King of Benguela*
> *who married the Princess*
> *to the Infant of Castille*

> *Bem bom bem bom*
> *furumaná furumaná*
> *Catulê cala montuê*
> *condembá*

These processions usually convene around a Negro church, bringing hundreds or perhaps thousands of people together in an atmosphere of tempestuous sound. The play tells the story of the death of the Queen's youngest son; driven to despair the Queen summons the magician and orders him to use his art to revive the child. The witch-doctor, dressed as befits his function, with serpents and iron chains for necklaces, dances around the child; from time to time he reaches into the bag he has slung over his shoulder and pulls out roots, resins, adders' teeth and other magical objects, and throws them at the child until at last the boy gives a great leap and joins the dance, while all around him the people rejoice and sing. It all reminded me of those Morality plays so popular back in the villages in our country at Christmastime, which depict the birth, death and resurrection of Jesus Christ.

And on the matter of death and resurrection, you can imagine how much I enjoyed learning that my tragic demise has also been reported in the Portuguese and French newspapers. It is a lucky man who can read his own obituary, especially when he is doing it in Paradise – and by that I'm not referring to that chilly cabinet of souls which modern theologians tell us about, but to the real Paradise, the classic Paradise, with tall palm trees and an indigo sea, passion-fruit liqueur, a woman – the Woman! – beautiful as an angel, but with all those other precious qualities which other angels always lack.

Saudades from your friend,
Fradique

Letter to Eça de Queiroz
Cajaíba Plantation, May 1877

My dear José Maria,

Last week there was a big party on my land. I decided to free all the workers on the plantation, which turned out to be a good pretext for a happy display of emancipatory enthusiasm, which brought some of the leading figures of the growing abolitionist movement up to São Francisco do Conde. Most of the workers have chosen to remain in my service, and I will be paying them the same as the European settlers get paid in the southern provinces, as well as taking responsibility for their health and the education of their children.

One of the few who chose not to stay was Córnelio, the old Hausa man I wrote to you about in my last letter: he came to me, very serious, full of the ancient pride of his race, and explained that he meant to return to Africa, and to visit Mecca, and then to die. 'The life of a slave', he told me, 'is a house with many windows but no door. The life of a free man is a house with many doors, but not a single window.' He had managed to save up a little over the last few years, making baskets which he sold in the village, and wanted me to help him to buy the crossing ticket. He showed me what he had managed to save (very little) and I told him that, yes, it was enough, and paid the difference out of my own pocket. He left yesterday – utterly serene – on the weekly barge that links this village to São Salvador. Ana Olímpia was still trying to dissuade him from going, alarmed at the folly of his venture, but he was immovable. 'After so many years,' my friend said to him, 'nobody will remember you in the land of the Hausa.' The old man shrugged. 'I'm not going there to look for other people,' he replied. 'I'm going to look for myself.'

For three days and three nights the Negroes danced and sang, ate and drank, around ten bonfires all over the broad yard that stretches out behind the Main House. At the same time we were also visited by a number of gentlemen who had travelled up from Salvador, Pernambuco and even Rio de Janeiro, to this lost port, on a sort of rowdy pilgrimage against slavery.

That was how I came to meet José do Patrocínio, a young journalist who I'm told is the terror of all the great plantation-owners. He has a pleasant face framed by a soft beard, his large eyes tender and honest; when he gets into discussion he seems to grow, he is transformed, until, inflamed by his own rhetoric, he looks like a tiger about to pounce. Doubtless the extraordinary vigour of his words and the studied theatricality of his gestures make him an extremely dangerous orator, one capable of arousing the excitement of multitudes. Politically he is pure Proudhon: 'Slavery is theft', he repeats often, in between long tirades against the coffee barons and The Holy Mother Church. Interestingly, his father was a priest, as well as a slave-owner and farmer; and his mother (a poor Creole Negress) sold fruit in Campos dos Goitacazes, a region to the east of Rio de Janeiro. Raised in the Campos presbytery and in a nearby farm, José left his parents' home when still a boy to work and study at the Misericórdia Hospital in Rio de Janeiro. Today you can hear young radicals declaiming articles he has been publishing in the *News Gazette* as if they were poetry – or prayer! And at the meetings of the numerous anti-slavery societies that are thriving all over the country, his name is spoken with something approaching reverence.

Another important figure in the emancipation movement had also travelled up from Rio with José do Patrocínio: the lawyer Luís Gama, very well known in recent years for his distinguished defence of citizens enslaved illegally. Gama has experience of this situation himself; born the son of a free black woman (and thus having the right to freedom) he was nevertheless sold by his father when still a child, before running away and living through an incredible series of adventures, eventually receiving his training and setting himself up as a lawyer. 'In us,' Gama told me, 'even our colour is a defect. An unforgivable evil of birth, the stigma of a crime. But our critics forget that this colour of ours is also the cause of the wealth of all those thousands of thieves who insult us; and that this colour associated with slavery, so like the colour of the earth itself, shelters volcanoes under its dark surface, volcanoes where the sacred fire of freedom burns.'

Speeches like this set him apart from certain other *mestizos*, who forget all about their African roots as soon as they become wealthy, and who do society the favour of allowing them to forget what they have done too. In his book *A Picturesque Voyage Across Brazil* the German painter Johann Moritz Rugendas records the reply of a man who was asked whether a certain Captain-Major was a mulatto. 'He used to be,' the man replied, 'but he isn't any more'. And seeing Rugendas' surprise at this apparent marvel his interlocutor went on: 'But, Sir, *can* a Captain-Major be a mestizo?'

Two days after all our guests had left – that is, last Friday – I was visited quite unexpectedly by an old friend and compatriot Alexandre Gomes (you might remember him?), who is now the owner of a cigar factory in Recife and who more than anyone encouraged me to buy this farm. Alexandre arrived arm in arm with a venerable-looking character, an old man with a long white beard, whom he introduced to me as the Baron of Rio das Contas, Frutuoso Vicente, owner of the neighbouring Paramirim Plantation. Both seemed a little concerned, and it didn't

take me long to discover why. They had come, Alexandre
explained, to warn me against the folly of opening up my
farm to a group of dangerous anarchists:

'You haven't been in Brazil long,' Alexandre said to me,
'and you know next to nothing about local politics. That
black man who was here, the one who calls himself José
do Patrocínio, is in the service of the most monstrous
interests . . .'

'He's a brigand!' shouted the Baron. 'He's worse than
an anarchist. He's a bandit who just wants to foment
insurrection by any means he can! Did Your Excellency
know that not only does he defend the emancipation of
slaves, but he also thinks that we should not have the
right to any compensation from the State?! If the State
cannot pay so many slaves itself, slaves which the State
itself sold and on which it has charged us taxes, then how
can *we* be expected to pay them?'

'This party of yours,' Alexandre continued, trying to
calm the Baron, 'this strange meeting that took place
here, and, even more serious than that, your ridiculous
decision to free your slaves – all this is very worrying to
respectable people.'

I could simply have thanked the two men for taking an
interest and changed the subject. That's what I was
expected to do. But Alexandre's final words, dropping the
subtle but poisonous hint of a threat, awoke in me the
long-contained rage of the Mendes:

'Respectable people? Respected by the Devil, perhaps!
How can people who feed themselves on other men's
bread be respectable people?'

You know my opinions on slavery. I'm sure that one of
these days Jesus Christ will return to earth, thoroughly
disgusted, and will free the slaves, and he will have his
prophets and his church. But then he will have to be
denied and crucified, and at last there will be new hordes

of slaves, all over again. It has always been thus, and always shall be, and there's nothing to be done about it. But at that moment, irritated at Alexandre's insolence, all I could remember was José do Patrocínio's maxim, stolen from old Proudhon:

'Slavery is theft!'

The Baron did not expect that (nor indeed did I). He turned very red, gripped the handle of his walking-stick tightly with trembling hands, and I was afraid that he might simply drop dead at my feet on the spot. But he managed to resist. Instead he drew himself upright, picked up his top hat, and without offering me his hand made for the door.

'Goodbye,' he muttered in a very slight voice. 'You'll hear of me yet.'

Alexandre followed him, shaking his head, and I watched them leave, becoming more and more certain that with that episode I had signed a declaration of war. And at the same moment I realized that I had just chosen my *class affiliation* (our beloved poet Antero de Quental was fond of that expression). That is, I think I found in this country a new cause to occupy my spirit and keep idleness at bay.

I'll bid you goodbye now, as it's getting late, and set off to meet History and the Revolution!

With my brotherly greetings,
Fradique

Letter to Eça de Queiroz
Rio de Janeiro, June 1877

My dear José Maria,

I received your letter at Cajaíba, together with the book and papers, all of which smelled strongly of smoke, of tar, of the sweat of the workers from dreadful Newcastle-upon-Tyne. You ask me how the Revolution is going – it is going dangerously! When (as old Fernão Mendes Pinto would say) *I cast my eyes over the many great works and dangers I encounter*, I find it hard to put them into any kind of order, to make of them any kind of sense, even to give them any credibility, which is something which our poor countryman never managed to do (by an agreeable irony 'old Fernão Mendes Pinto' is an anagram of 'And men of prose don't lie'!).

I am now in Rio de Janeiro, and leave on Monday for Lisbon where I mean to stay a month or two before going on to Paris and then London. There are obvious reasons for this little pilgrimage of mine (business to deal with and friends to see), but other less public ones too: I have recently become attached to a secret anti-slavery society (we call it the Termite Society!) and I'm travelling to try to gather support for this cause from the governments and institutions of old Europe. I will be relying on your help and that of our friends, as I find myself in possession of some documents which, when published, cannot but cause a scandal of the greatest magnitude.

But (I can already hear you say) we will never be able to topple the coffee barons that way. No, my sceptical friend, you're quite right about that. We won't be able to defeat them with shame, nor even with ridicule, but we can at least prevent them from wandering the Champs Elysées with the tranquillity of the righteous. I should say that Brazilians nurture a real obsession for the City of

Light. In Rio de Janeiro, on the Rua do Ouvidor, you find the dazzling shop-windows of the fashion houses, like 'Notre Dame de Paris' or 'O Grande Magico', the florists and the fine pâtisseries, and in these splendid places you won't hear a word spoken that is not in French, and always spoken with that same cursory but assured manner with which the master of ceremonies back in Luanda would lead the dancing of the *rebita*.

What would a wealthy Brazilian landowner want all his power for if he can't exercise it freely in his beloved Paris? What good are the top-hat and monocle to him, the gold watch and the foppish suit, if he can't parade himself happily in them at the very latest Charles Garnier opera, or the classic Odéon? To the Brazilian aristocracy, both the legitimate and the coffee-money aristocracy, Paris is like the magic mirror to the wicked witch: 'Mirror, mirror, on the wall . . .' Frutuoso Vicente asks the French capital, 'Who is the richest man of all?' The coffee baron's life depends on the answer to this question, for only if he exists in Paris can he be sure that he exists at all.

Are you laughing? Do you think I'm exaggerating? I myself only recently understood the extent of these men's power and their madness, and how important to them are those papers I'm bringing with me. It was about four in the afternoon, and I was crossing from Niteroi to Rio by boat, alone, absorbing the incomparable landscape that was unfolding in front of me. These steam boats, identical at bow and stern to allow them to moor from both sides, have two classes, one for those of us in shoes, the other for those going barefoot – that is, one for gentlemen and another for slaves – with us (those in shoes) travelling in a spacious, comfortable saloon. You can buy newspapers on the boat, so that anyone growing tired of admiring the marvellous view this trip offers can always occupy his time with the paper, studying the minuscule intrigues at Court instead. The twenty-minute crossing slips by easily and pleasantly, and unless the sea is very rough you never notice the time passing.

The boat was almost empty. Looking out at the magnificent green hills in the distance, breaking out from between the vast patchwork of clustered houses, I was sadly contemplating the destiny of Man, the imperfections of the world and how much I miss the practical experience of my faithful Smith. At this point I noticed a thin, dark little chap with a moustache and goatee beard sitting very upright opposite me. He had a newspaper open on his lap which he was pretending to read (it was this that drew my attention to him, the certainty that he wasn't really reading his paper). He raised his eyes and looked directly at me.

'I hope your Excellency will pardon me,' he said with a nasal, bovine voice, heavy with a north-eastern accent, 'but I think we've met before somewhere.'

'It's possible', I replied, doubtful. 'I'm there often.'

He ignored my little joke.

'But I do want to be sure. Aren't you the Portuguese man, Fradique Mendes?'

I had a bad premonition and was on my feet in a flash, and at that moment the man stood up, put his hand in his jacket and pointed a pistol at me:

'May his Lordship forgive me,' he said. 'God knows that it will not be me who kills you . . .'

The agility which I acquired through years of fencing saved me. I jumped aside, heard the shot, the quick whistle of the bullet, and hurled myself at the gunman. He lost his balance, dropped the revolver and ran along the deck knocking over an unfortunate old man, then without a second's hesitation flung himself into the water. Two sailors threw themselves at me, blocking my way, and suddenly the saloon was full of a confused crowd of people shouting and I found myself being dragged before the captain. Back on land I spent three long hours trying to persuade the diligent harbour police that there could be no explanation for the man's behaviour – a man I'd never seen in my life! – but a sudden attack of insanity.

Later I went to visit José do Patrocínio, about whom I think I've already spoken to you – a journalist, one of the outstanding names in the anti-slavery movement. My friend listened in silence to my account of my strange adventure. I told him everything, just as I'm telling you now, including the gunman's last words to me. Patrocínio shook his head, concerned:

'A Procurer-of-Christ! These people have gone crazy! . . .'

'Procurer-of-Christ' is the peculiar name by which pro-fessional assassins are known in the north-east of this country. When these gunmen have a job proposed to them, they go to Mass with their *Mandante*, the man who has commissioned the murder, and at that solemn moment when the priest raises the Host they receive the agreed salary and the bullet with which they are to do the job. Through this ritual the assassins believe that they have been absolved of responsibility for the crime, since Christ saw them from the altar, witnessed the agreement and recorded the *Mandante*'s face. The Procurers-of-Christ, so José do Patrocínio tells me, rarely fail to deliver on a mission: convinced of their innocence and the sacred nature of the contract they have entered into, and tied to an idea of honour which will make no allowance for fail-ure or betrayal, they will do anything necessary to achieve what has been asked of them.

In the opinion of my good friend, the gunman will make another attempt to kill me, to shoot or stab me, and so I ought to be ready to face him. Against my wishes Patrocínio sought out two well-known *capoeira* fighters,

called Cobrinha Verde and João Sossego[4] – the names well
fitting their respective owners – and gave them strict
instructions to remain close to me at all times, which
indeed they do, following me about wherever I go: I stop
for a moment to look into a shop window and five metres
behind me I can make out my two shadows; I go into a
tobacconist's and they wait for me at the door, scratching
their bare feet and looking with fierce suspicion at anyone
who follows me inside. Yesterday I tried to escape, breaking into a run and plunging into the confusion of people
in the Rua do Ouvidor – shouting newspaper-vendors,
gentlemen in pleasant conversation, slow ladies with
their domestic slave-girls – and all I managed to do was
provoke utter chaos, since a group of young men (seeing
me apparently running away from two *capoeiras*) decided
to come to my rescue. Cobrinha Verde and João Sossego
confronted us, and with headbutts, trip-ups, and other
elaborate kinds of attack that make up their art soon dispersed them all. The three of us then fled, ahead of two
urbanos (local policemen), like common criminals, during
which I lost my hat, my walking-stick and five centuries
of self-possessed Mendes dignity.

By now I'm sure you can tell for yourself quite how
dangerous this revolution has become.

Your loving friend,
Fradique

---

4 Literally, 'Little Green Cobra' and 'John Peace' – DH.

EUROPE

Letter to Ana Olímpia
Saragoça Estate, July 1877

My love,

I bought Cajaíba Island because I wanted to give you – well, perhaps not Paradise exactly, but at least a temporary port of shelter, and when we said our goodbyes in May I still thought that such a thing was possible. I was wrong. I'm writing with the most serious news, dreadful in itself but also a matter of concern regarding its implications for your safety. A few days before leaving for Lisbon a man tried to shoot me on the little boat that ferries people between Rio and the town of Niteroi; he managed to escape and swim to safety. I wasn't particularly alarmed by this, as I have some very high-calibre enemies around and am quite used to their expressions of dislike – even including gunshots! I described what had happened to me to José do Patrocínio, and suspecting that the man might be a professional assassin he hired two *capoeiras* to protect me. So I spent the rest of the week trying to escape from Patrocínio's men and wasn't able to get shot of them until Monday when I finally boarded the boat that was to take me to Lisbon.

It was raining. There were fine drops of water suspended in the air, that kind of melancholy, tiresome little rain the Portuguese call a *molha-tontos*, an idiot-wetter. I spent a long time on deck, watching Brazil disappear sadly into the mist, then went in search of my cabin. There, set out in a corner, I found a trunk almost identical to my own. At first I thought myself the victim of some insignificant mistake, an everyday case of misdirected baggage, the sort of thing that happens to all travellers from time to time and which is soon resolved. But I noticed in a moment that the name on the case was my own. Nervously I opened it, and what I saw took my breath away: looking straight at me, with cold glass eyes, was the stuffed head of a black man.

I closed the case again. It felt like a horrible, squalid nightmare: I was nauseous, and felt the ship spinning on the ocean – I unfastened the porthole and lay down in my hammock. I don't know how long I remained like that, breathing hard the heavy, humid air, until my nerves had calmed. I got up and opened the case again. The head was still there and only then, with the most intense horror, did I recognize the noble features of old Cornélio.

I know that this news will upset you. You can imagine how it upset me. The killing of old Cornélio is all the more vile a crime, all the more absurd, for the fact that there is no doubt that it was committed with the sole purpose of frightening us, of mocking us. And alas with the theft of my own trunk I have lost those documents with which I was hoping to rouse Europe from her old-lady's slumber and give that whole rabble of slave-owners and traders who are against the development of Brazil a fierce shaking-up. We've lost! But we have lost just one battle, for this war has barely begun.

I threw Cornélio's head in the sea. It was a heavy, moonless night off the Cape Verde Islands. Iemanjá, the *quiandas*, all the powerful divinities of Africa's hot waters will accompany his spirit back to the land of the Hausa. Cornélio never allowed himself to be enslaved: even tied to a whipping-post, even chained to the foot of the highest walls, his soul was always free. Now at last he will find his way back home.

I promise this horrific crime will not go unpunished. You and I and our friends, we will avenge Cornélio's death. But I beg you not to make any overt protest. Tell Ernesto to put men on guard around the farm, day and night; try to avoid going out, and if you do make sure you're never alone and always careful.

I love you.
Fradique

Letter to Ana Olímpia
Saragoça Estate, August 1877

My love,

Your letter has given me new courage: it cleaned out my tired soul, just like the November rains clean the dust from off the African roads. I wish I had the Count of Cagliostro's idol with me (our Count, the one from the *Nação Crioula*), here with his mysterious art, just so that I could ask him every day, every moment, how you are and what you are doing. Here on my estate at Saragoça, hiding away from the deadly heat that suffocates the capital, I do nothing but walk and contemplate and, of course, think of you.

A week ago I went with Eça de Queiroz for a cod dinner at Mouraria, in a little tavern he worships with well-merited (extremely well-merited!) fervour. He has been exiled for nearly four years now to Newcastle-upon-Tyne where, for the good of the nation, he wastes away and he writes, and now he has come to Lisbon in search of our old Portugal. He found no traces of the heroic land of Camões, neither in Rossio nor in Chiado, and then – almost losing faith – he remembered Mouraria and its tavern. The two of us went together, and there we truly found Portugal, as she sat among the vagrants and fish-wives, singing a *fado*, with an overwhelming stench of garlic and sweat about her. The cod arrived – marvellous – with chickpeas, peppers and fresh salsa, and we fell silent in celebration of so great a moment. It was already past midnight by the time we left, exhausted but reinvigorated, belching out the motherland, and just a little dizzy owing to the excellence of the red wine.

I had rented a room at the Hotel Bragança and made my way there in a carriage, after having left José Maria at the home of his aged parents at Rossio. In the hotel reception I heard a voice calling after me, a voice I thought I recognized, but when I turned I couldn't see anybody at all. That is, not until a tiny black figure in a black cassock jumped out from behind a heap of cases and trunks – Father Nicolau dos Anjos:

'I've never seen a dead man looking so well!' he shouted. 'Get those bones over here . . .'

I knelt down and the little man threw himself into my arms. He had arrived from Angola just a few hours earlier, and was to set off for the Vatican the following day. Finding me there, alive, made him excited and emotional.

'I prayed so much for your soul,' he said. 'In Luanda everyone thinks you're dead.'

As he said this he felt my arms, making absolutely sure that it was really me he was addressing and not merely my spirit. He asked after you, he wanted to know what had become of young Arcénio, then he dragged me to the tea-room where we stayed, almost till daybreak, exchanging news. That was how I came to know that Jesuíno Vaz de Caminha is prospering in Luanda, stealing a great deal (which has earned him great authority and responsibility), brutalizing the poor and fawning upon the rich. The priest swears that Gabriela Santamarinha is uglier than ever (which I don't believe possible!), and so far gone in her madness that no one will have any more to do with her now.

Nicolau dos Anjos set out from Luanda at the express summons of the Pope himself. His Holiness must have heard of the many wonders which our common friend has been carrying out (so carelessly) all across the backwoods of Angola, and become concerned and irritated. I wasn't told this by the unhappy Nicolau himself, of course, but that was what I was able to conclude from his silences and half-words. Old Pius IX knows that we live in the century of light, of science, of scepticism, and that for the Church to be modern it must break its links to the

Miracle, to its distant past of catacombs and magic. For the Church to be up-to-date it must not allow sorcerers to wander about in its name, reviving the dead, restoring the blind their sight, multiplying loaves or turning water into fresh *quissângua*; these things were acceptable 2,000 years ago, and not just acceptable but even admirable, but today they undermine the seriousness and good name of the great institutions (nobody expects a devout Queen Victoria to walk barefoot on the waters of the Thames!).

So Nicolau dos Anjos has been called to the Vatican because His Holiness would rather he were a little less virtuous, less worthy of the people's affection. His Holiness would rather he stayed far removed from the world, and even Benguela is too close for him (perhaps he will be sent to Pernambuco!).

Talking of miracles, one happened to me not long ago, or rather I was able with my own eyes (and my incredulous soul) to witness one occurring. I was going up the Rua do Ouro, alone, as night was starting to fall, when behind me I heard a sudden hubbub of horses' hooves and cries and turned to see a chariot racing out of control, the coachman in panic, filling the air with curses and cracks of his whip. There was a man in the horses' path trying to get away, but with so little agility that he would certainly have been run over had I not come to his aid: without a second thought I lunged forward and threw myself at the poor wretch, rolling on to the floor with him as the carriage passed over us and stopped, no further harm done, at the end of the street. The two of us got to our feet, shaking off the dust, and only then as I looked more closely at him did I realize that he was none other than that damnable, mercenary murderer, the Procurer-of-Christ who had tried to kill me in Rio de Janeiro.

'What the hell are you doing here?' I asked, stunned. 'Are you going to kill me . . .?'

The man, a dark little figure, with his moustache drooping and rough goatee, looked at me solemnly:

'I was,' he said in his ox-voice. 'I was, but I'm not going to any more.'

In the same tone, with his sing-song north-eastern accent, he explained to me that since I had saved his life he felt acquitted of his promise to kill me. 'God willed it this way,' he added. With no very good idea of what to say to him, I dragged him to a nearby bar, asked them to draw two beers, and settled down to hear the villain out. He didn't wait to be asked. Asdrúbal was the name he was given at the baptismal font, but in Limoeiro Velho, in the district of Escada, where he was born, they just call him The Boy. The godson of a wealthy plantation-owner, a certain Belmiro (by birth the Baron of Escada), he grew up wanting for nothing and even learnt to read and write.

He might have turned out to be a peaceable clerk; but one hot January afternoon, as he rode with this Belmiro, another rider burst out from the bush, a rifle in his hand and firing shots. Asdrúbal was just thirteen but already carried a gun. He drew his pistol and fired, bringing the other man down with his very first shot. And from then on Belmiro, impressed with the boy's skill and *sang froid*, took to using him whenever he found someone in his way; and so began a great career.

Asdrúbal, The Boy, told me all this as he drank his beer. His bovine voice held not a shadow of remorse. I wanted to know who had contracted him to kill me, but the villain just shrugged his shoulders: 'a friend of my godfather's. I've no idea what he's called.' I asked him whether his godfather or his godfather's friend knew that he was in Lisbon. Again he shrugged: 'No. When I learnt that you had left I decided to leave too. A week later I managed to get a job helping in the galley of a Portuguese brig and that was how I managed to get to Lisbon. I've been searching for you all this time but didn't find you till today. I was about to kill you when that carriage appeared.' He paused, drank another gulp, then looked me in the eye and murmured sadly:

'Now I cannot kill you, and I am dishonoured. I don't know what I should do.'

I felt sorry for the man:

'I'm most terribly sorry I saved you,' I said. 'If I had known it was you I wouldn't have done a thing.'

I ordered another two beers and on we went, drinking and talking, until the owner came with his apologies to ask us to let him close the place up. We bade farewell like old friends, and five days later he set off again, bound back to Brazil. As for me, I leave for France in two weeks.

I want you to think seriously about my proposal, and that you come out to join me. My friends from the Geographical Society were delighted at the idea of a conference on slave-trading and the predicament of Negroes in Brazil to be introduced by a woman who has felt (and still feels) the horror of that regime in her own skin.

Write to me to Paris.

From he who loves you –
Fradique

Letter to Ana Olímpia
Paris, September 1877

My sweet Princess,

I've just received your latest cheerful letter. So you are really coming! So in just a month I will be alive again. I'm afraid Paris doesn't deserve you, though. And it certainly isn't worth the storm of feelings you describe in your letter. Paris, the centre of civilization? Yes, of course! But what is civilization? Between the melancholy gentleman who frequents the salons of Madame de Jouarre, my kind godmother, and the distant cannibal of the Upper Amazon, there is no great difference of morality – only of gastronomy.

I've got the latest issue of the *Revue de Médecine* in front of me which contains the following article, which I thought very *à propos*: a murderer by the name of Bruno Sanjuan was guillotined on the night of April 24th and his body (which his family refused to receive) was donated to medical science, in the person of Professor Jupin. This gentleman rushed him into a carriage which had been converted into a travelling laboratory, into which he had already set up two lighted lanterns, an electric battery and a live dog (a Newfoundland). '*In this way,*' the magazine explains, '*Professor Jupin was able to conduct a number of very significant experiments of great scientific consequence on the way from the gibbet to the Laboratory Building.*'

The professor began by passing an electric current through Sanjuan's head while simultaneously blowing into his ears – with no result whatsoever. But when he increased the current the mouth began to open and shut as if the wretch still wanted to breathe. So the doctors carried out a blood transfusion from the dog to the head of the guillotined man and at the very first doses the face began to colour and there was slight contraction in the muscles. When the electric current was passed to the eyelids they flickered, and the eyes kept opening and closing for twenty or thirty seconds. When addressed by name the deceased turned his gaze towards the voice addressing him, giving the professor the impression that he had recognized him: '*He looked at me with loathing,*' the professor affirmed: '*It was with the same bitterness with which some days earlier he had received me in his cell.*' By now a full forty-five minutes had passed since the head and its body had been separated.

It would have been interesting to interview Sanjuan to find out, for example, what he was thinking as he turned his gaze on Professor Jupin, with the blood of a Newfoundland reanimating his brain. Would he be thinking 'Where the hell is my head?' Would he – more poetically – be remembering the wheatfields of his childhood? Or, more likely (if we remember the wise man's testimony – '*He looked at me with loathing*') would he have been thinking about committing murder? But how? Perhaps with his teeth: 'Get a little closer, Professor', he would beg, his voice frail, then *slash*, he would tear through his carotid artery.

So what was he thinking about? We will never know: alas, science has not yet got that far. Warily the gallant Professor Jupin merely concluded that it was not possible for a head to survive separation from its body.

Does my story horrify you, Princess? It's true! It is the true face of the civilization that awaits you. But don't be afraid to come. I will be here to protect you. I am, I will be always, your guardian angel.

Fradique

Letter to Eça de Queiroz
Paris, November 1877

My dear José Maria,

The other day an entomologist friend of mine told me that for a beehive to produce a kilo of honey it must gather pollen from five million flowers. Thinking of this extraordinary effort I have been wondering how many books Baudelaire had to read, how many lives he had to live, to write a single line of poetry. I have still read little, and contrary to what you claim I have not yet lived enough to pen so much as a sonnet, still less a novel or – worse still – 'my memoirs'. It was Baudelaire himself who wrote *'Le temps mange la vie, / Et l'obscur ennemi qui nous ronge le coeur / Du sang que nous perdons croît et se fortifie.'*

At one point in your last letter you questioned whether the characters I have been telling you about are authentic, and hence deduced that I had already been 'creating literature'. But do you really think me (or indeed anyone) capable of creating, for example, the figure of a dreaming, miracle-working Negro dwarf priest? Nothing but Reality, in its vertiginous and unsurpassable lunacy, would dare to dream up such wonders.

No, I don't create literature. And I have no intention of writing my memoirs, now or at any time in the future. The most interesting things to happen in my life have always been the lives of other people. Take the case of my friend Ana Olímpia, who though a Princess by right was forced to be a slave, then a slave-owner, and is today one of the foremost campaigners against the slave trade. At the moment she is visiting us in Paris. A week ago scores of people gathered at the Geographical Society to hear her speak. Ana Olímpia told the story of the drama of her childhood; she recalled her father, a Congolese king who spent years dying in a Luandan jail; she evoked the dark early mornings when, accompanied by her mother, she would stand at the docks and watch the departure of the slave ships for Brazil. All the speeches of all the abolitionists in all Europe are not worth as much as testimony like hers. And do you know why? Because the splendid light of truth shines in everything Ana Olímpia says, while in the mouths of our well-meaning philanthropists nothing burns but the dim lamp of rhetoric. It is the distance spanning the gulf between Life and literature. And I prefer Life.

On that subject, I think it'd be worth taking advantage of Ana Olímpia's visit to Europe to take her to London. I'm sure our friends in the Abolitionist Society would be delighted. I imagine that as a representative of the Crown you can't get involved in this matter, one which is so awkward for Portugal and Brazil, and I would never ask such a thing of you. But I do have something else to ask: merely that you keep your superiors informed about this and every abolitionist lecture. Send them panic-mongering accounts daily, which show how the question of slavery dominates public opinion in the United Kingdom. Tell them it is imperative that they take urgent measures to eliminate what is left of Negro trafficking. Insinuate that a British fleet is considering a total blockade of Brazil. Tell them that there are rumours of a boycott of Port wine. In short, pester them, terrorize them!

A young lawyer by the name of Joaquim Nabuco, who is currently in the Brazilian delegation to Washington, became famous in 1869 when he had to defend a slave in Recife who had already once been condemned to the gallows. Tomás (the slave) had been publicly whipped, and in reprisal had murdered his master. Condemned to death, he managed to escape from prison, killing a guard in the process. He was soon recaptured and brought again to trial, and it fell to Nabuco to defend him.

'This man has committed no crime!' shouted Nabuco, pointing at the slave. 'He simply removed an obstacle in his path!' The public present began to perk up at once, and the young lawyer proceeded to denounce the brutality and absurdity of slavery:

'A man who fights against the agencies of punishment is in a way making his own personal defence against a judicial order which neither respects him nor protects him.'

Tomás was condemned to life imprisonment, but at least avoided the gallows. And this principle of legitimate defence used by Nabuco made history, and came to be quoted as a precedent in similar cases. It is because I believe in it myself (and there is not much else I do believe in) that I have come together with all those who are fighting against slavery.

I hope to see you soon. And yes, then we really can talk about literature. Your affectionate friend,

Fradique

Letter to Ana Olímpia
Paris, April 1878

My Princess,

I've just had a letter from Arcénio de Carpo in which he inadvertently reveals information he supposed me already to be aware of. And shouldn't I have been? If only like a worm I could have five hearts, then I would have one heart celebrating, another would be tight with anguish, the third enraged, the fourth would be questioning the world and the fifth, simply, burning with passion. But in my single heart all these emotions become jumbled, and being violently confused they produce in me a state of general excitement which I have no power to control or even to define.

So I am to be a father, and you hid the news from me. Arcénio writes that the child is due in July. That means that when we parted in February you were already carrying my son in your belly, hidden from me. It is true that I did not mean to have children; I remember that we discussed the matter and disagreed. I told you then that I wanted no trace of my passage through this world left behind me apart from a faint, vague nostalgia settling on the places, the people, the objects that once I loved passionately. A man has a child, and then what happens? Soon this child gives him two grandchildren, and they in turn four great-grandchildren, and so on, originating a noisy torrent of people who will carry your name and your blood on through eternity. Making a child is creating a whole universe. There will be angels, but there will be devils too; there will be love, but also hatred; and along with the sublime will come the abominable. As someone who doesn't find the role of God to be particularly appealing, a child seems to me (seemed, seemed) to be an act of the greatest arrogance and temerity.

I do indeed remember having defended this view, after

dinner, little knowing that you were carrying a child of mine. But – good God! – it was after dinner and we were just talking. Convinced that I would never produce off-spring, I smoked and I philosophized. Had I known your condition I would doubtless have philosophized quite the contrary case, and with just as much conviction, if not more.

In short, these brief lines are just to tell you that I will be in Recife in thirty or forty days. I'm leaving earlier than expected, not only because of young Arcénio's letter, but also because without you this city seems dead to me, and I feel unbearably lonely. As old Balzac wrote (was it Balzac?): solitude is best, so long as you have someone with whom to talk about it. I embrace you, and our child.

Fradique

BRAZIL

Letter to Madame de Jouarre
Cajaíba Plantation, October 1878

My dear godmother,

The man who is writing you this letter is no longer the idle and irresponsible adventurer you watched growing up, having himself dressed by the best tailors in Paris in order to conceal the wretched nakedness of his soul, thinking with borrowed ideas, experiencing the world with other people's feelings, a man whose only ambition was simply to get on with his life. I am an entirely new man! I am, as of two months ago, the father of a beautiful girl whom I have called Sophia in your honour. I was never able to understand the mania for procreation, that compulsion on which the great social movements invariably depend, and on which theologies, philosophies and sacred mysteries are based. I still can't. Yet I am a father now, and in some strange way I feel as though this child is my future, and the reason for my past.

Sophia's birth gave us the pretext for a big party which brought dozens of people together in this house. We had visitors from Rio, including the journalist José do Patrocínio, the lawyer Luís Gama, the engineer André Rebouças, all important names in the anti-slavery movement; Manuel Querino, a wise Bahian man, came too, from a town not far from here. I think he is probably the first Brazilian historian to take an interest in the future of the slaves in this country. For years he has been studying the rituals, the festivities, the art and cuisine of the Negroes. He believes that Brazil's originality (that is, its very nationality) is essentially a result of this African influence and the mixing of races.

While the theoreticians of human inequality, men like Joseph Gobineau, denounce the corruption of European blood in South America and prophesy the continent's impending decline, our Bahian looks at the world from the stoop of his little house over in Matatú Grande, and phlegmatically proclaims the birth of a new man and a new civilization. As you have doubtless guessed, Querino is himself a mulatto, and he believes that it is the people of his race who will one day take control of Brazil. What he has yet to understand is that with the end of the slave trade and as a result of the consequent increase in the number of European and mixed-blood settlers, this country will be entirely white within four or five generations. So the abolition of slavery is signalling the beginning of the end for the black man in Brazil. The dances will stay, perhaps, and we will still see white-skinned ladies practising their belly-thrusts as they spin to the drum-music; the old African gods will survive too, worshipped by a people who have quite forgotten about Africa herself, and slavery itself will remain too as a vague, distant memory. But the rest will be just ash and shadows.

We were also joined by two old acquaintances of mine, two exceedingly dangerous *capoeiras* who served as my protection when I visited Rio de Janeiro last June on my way through to Lisbon. As you might remember, at the time I was carrying certain documents which were somewhat inconvenient to the Brazilian slaving-world and José do Patrocínio felt I would be safer if I were accompanied. Cobrinha Verde and João Sossego (those are the two *capoeiras'* names) are here now as protection for

Patrocínio himself. This journalist, who has a price on his head all across the north-east, where the plantation-owners loathe him and the slaves and freed-men worship him, arrived here swarmed about by dancing and singing crowds – I'm not sure the Emperor himself would have been so well received.

In my house I keep a old copy of the *Illustrated London News*, dated 1848, an edition which is devoted exclusively to the French Revolution. One of the pictures shows a vast barricade on top of which a group of rebels is parading. At the foot of the barricade is a small sign saying 'No vacancies'. Nowadays in Brazil the trenches of the fight against slavery are likewise packed to bursting. The young people of the main cities in the Empire have finally woken up to the horror of a regime which their fathers thought was eternal (and blessed by The Creator) and more or less everywhere there are now marches, meetings and societies springing up in favour of abolition.

To me it is obvious that the system of slavery must be torn down by the children of the slave-owners, just as it was the children of the colonizers (and not the Indians) who declared independence, not just here in Brazil but all over the Americas. For José do Patrocínio, however, it is the blacks and the mulattos who must lead this revolution, and Ana Olímpia feels the same way. Only yesterday she said to me 'If we are offered our freedom by the white men, then we will never be truly free. We have to conquer our freedom ourselves if we are then to be able to face you as equals.' Following this logic she defended the continuation of the fighting between the races. I was startled: 'But what about us? What will happen to us?' My friend laughed: 'We will fight, and I'll win!'

I fear Sophia may be like her mother. Aged three months she is already screaming for her rights, and with such vigour that she scares away birds and frightens dogs;

I'm afraid that with practice she may even attain the power of the mythological Reuben, Jacob's first-born, whose cries caused those who heard them to die of shock. Sophia is a strong, healthy child with big, intense dark eyes, alive to the world around them, and a confident smile, the smile of one who is readying herself to conquer the world. And conquer it she shall.

With *saudades* from your godson,

Fradique

EUROPE

Letter to Eça de Queiroz
Paris, October 1888

My dear José Maria,

My answer is no. No, I cannot write an article on 'The Current Situation of Portugal in Africa' for your magazine. And in brief (since I can already see you enraged, just about to draw your gun!) I'll explain why.

I'm afraid, my friend, that it's not in Portugal's interests that the world should know the situation in our colonies at this moment. We Portuguese are only in Africa because of forgetfulness – the forgetfulness of our government and the forgetfulness of the great powers. Any noise, even the slightest whisper in a little article in the *Revista de Portugal*, and we run the risk of the English discovering that the Portuguese territory of Zambezia has no sign of the Portuguese in it whatsoever, and before we know where we are we will have lost Zambezia altogether.

So you see my silence is a patriotic one. If we stay quiet and still, then perhaps the world, unaware that we aren't in the Congo, in Zambezia or Guinea, will allow us to carry on not being there.

Incidentally, the Portuguese presence in Africa reminds me of an episode that happened not long ago. While I was visiting my plantation at Cajaíba a man rode past me on horseback. He was practically lying down, half-slipping off, just letting himself be taken by the animal, his hat fallen over his eyes, and for a moment I wondered if he was dead or asleep. 'Amazing!' I remarked to Ana Olímpia, 'have you seen how that man is sitting on his horse?'

'Sitting?' my friend asked, astonished. 'You can hardly call that sitting! He looks as though he has just been dropped on top of it! . . .'

I think of that rider as being like Portugal riding Africa. No, not riding it, just dropped there. Our presence in Africa doesn't obey any principle, any idea, nor does it look as though it will have any end other than the pillaging of the Africans. And once dropped into Africa the unfortunate Portuguese try in the first place to keep themselves in the saddle – that is, alive and thieving – little caring in which direction the continent is headed. And Portugal, having once dropped them there, has forgotten all about them. Some of the long-forgotten settlers in turn forget all about their old homeland and go native. They are the happiest. They delve into the bushlands ('God is great,' they say, 'but the bush is greater'), and just as they change their trousers and shirts for animal hides, they abandon the Portuguese language, or use it in tatters mixed up with the resonant languages of Africa.

In his book *Across Africa*, Verney Lovett Cameron recounts an event which illustrates this well. He describes how not long after arriving in Benguela a native-born white official came to find him and offered to hand over the city and fort to him if the British administration would be prepared to include meat in their diet three times a week, rather than the one portion they were then being allowed. Cameron, embarrassed, declined. If only he had accepted, I'm sure we would have seen our generals in Lisbon offering the English the island of Madeira, or perhaps the city of Porto, or Douro and its vineyards, in exchange for a daily portion of meat, some fruit and a sweet for dessert, and perhaps a cup of coffee.

And what is it exactly that we have colonized? Brazil, you'll say. Not even that. We colonized Brazil with the slaves we went to round up in Africa, we had children with them, and Brazil then colonized itself. We spent four long centuries building up an empire – a vast empire, certainly, but unfortunately an imaginary one. To make it into a reality would take far more than just our consoling southern fantasy. England and France, cerebral and materialistic countries that they are, don't understand – will never understand – the pure and entirely unsentimental abstraction that leads an entire people to affirm (as they run their hand proudly over the map of the world): 'it is ours!' And it is no longer with the maternal Spain but with England, with France and with Germany that we now have to struggle if we are to colonize Africa.

Constructing a Portuguese Africa would require no less than Portugal herself becoming African. I'd even dare to suggest – as an essential first step – that the capital of the kingdom should be moved to Luanda, together with the King and his Court, the Chamber of Deputies, all the Ministries and, of course, the sweet pastries of Belém. The second phase would have to see the moving over of the Portuguese people, even the virtuous and the workers, with the criminals currently serving terms of exile in Angola and Mozambique being transferred up to Portugal. And then Portugal, as a small and by-and-large depopulated territory, could then be governed by some *empacaceiro* on a temporary secondment.

Our politicians are very fond of saying that we are in Africa to civilize the savages and spread the messages of Christianity. Nonsense! The Portuguese caravels were motivated only by the biological impulse to propagate the race. We are in Africa, in the Americas and in the East for the same reason that fungi scatter their spores and rabbits copulate – because deep down we know (our blood knows) that colonization means survival! The rage which drove Genghis Khan and his prodigious cavalcade across Mongolia, from Korea to the Urals, is just the same that today helps us to understand the dissemination of Koch's bacillus. All living beings are imperialistic. To live is to colonize.

But, alas, Portugal doesn't really colonize, it just spreads. That is how we are as a nation, a rather less sophisticated lifeform than Koch's bacillus. And worse still: some strange perversity means that wherever the Portuguese manage to get to (and we have got quite far), not only do they forget their civilizing – that is, colonizing – mission, but they quickly allow themselves to be colonized – that is, decivilized – by the local people.

When he stepped on to the land of Vera Cruz, Pero Vaz de Caminha immediately confessed his admiration for the Indians (in particular the Indian women): *'they don't plough, nor cultivate crops. There are no oxen here, no cows or goats, no sheep, chickens or any other kind of livestock which you usually find men living off. They only eat yams (of which there are a great deal), those seeds and fruit which trees have allowed to drop to the ground naturally. And just like this they are able to be so well off, better even than us, however much wheat and vegetables we might eat.'*

It was rather a case of the ant becoming envious of the grasshopper. It is hardly surprising that when his fleet left for its return to Lisbon, it left behind not just the exiles but also two cabin-boys, *'who tonight took flight, leaving the ship in a rowing-boat, and who will not be coming back.'* And I have no doubt that the whole of the crew would also have stayed, lazing about and enjoying the yams and fruit and seeds, not to mention the Indian women, had it not been for their fear of Pedro Álvares Cabral and King Don Manuel I.

So there you have them, in brief, my reasons why even now I will not add my name to that illustrious list of contributors to the *Revista de Portugal*.

I await your news, and your forgiveness.

Your friend,
Fradique

'Thus, filled with ideas, with delicate operations and good works, passed the final years of Fradique Mendes, in Paris, until the winter of 1888 when death came to fetch him away, in just the way that he (like Caesar) had always wanted, inopinatam ataque repentinam. *(. . .) According to Dr Labert, it was an extremely rare form of pleurisy. And he added, with perfect feeling for human happiness: 'Toujours de la chance, ce Fradique.'*

Eça de Queiroz, in
The Correspondence of Fradique Mendes

ANGOLA

Letter from Sra Ana Olímpia, trader in Angola,
To the Portuguese writer Eça de Queiroz
Luanda, August 1900

Esteemed Sir,

I fear you might not remember me. In 1888 I received a letter from you informing me that you were planning to publish a collection of the correspondence of Carlos Fradique Mendes, and asking me whether I would be prepared to help you with that project. It was, you wrote, *'a kind of tribute to the most interesting Portuguese man of the nineteenth century'*, as well as an act of patriotism, *'as in these times of uncertainty and bitterness we must not let Portuguese figures like this be forgotten, far away, lost beneath the muteness of a slab of marble.'* In my reply I said that I thought Carlos would have wanted that exactly, that once dead he should remain dead, and far away, and lost beneath the muteness of that marble slab. Some months later as I flicked through the Rio de Janeiro *News Gazette* I discovered that you had chosen to disregard my opinion.

You were right to do so. At the time, it's true, I thought the idea a repellent one. The publication of those letters seemed to me a kind of profanation, the perverse action of a necrophile. Carlos Fradique Mendes, exposed like a cadaver on a cold slab in an anatomical museum, still himself, perhaps himself, and yet irremediably someone else – a naked corpse, lying on his back exposed to the voracious indiscretion of the masses.

Years have gone by, I have grown old, I've re-read those old newspapers and the letters that Carlos wrote me, and bit by bit I have come to understand that you were right. Fradique doesn't belong to us, those who loved him, any more than the sky belongs to the birds that fly in it. His letters can be read as chapters of an inexhaustible novel, or of several novels, and in that sense they belong to humanity itself. Those letters which I am sending you, selected from the many Fradique wrote me over the course of twenty years (and to which I'm also attaching some addressed to Madame de Jouarre which she recently passed on to me) tell a story which in itself might seem a little extraordinary to your European readers. It is not the story of my life. It is the story of my life as told by Fradique Mendes. I hope you will be able to grasp the difference.

I saw Carlos Fradique Mendes for the first time one grey evening in May 1868 on the Luanda docks. I had just turned eighteen and knew the world only through books. Naturally, though, I thought I did know it. My husband, Victorino Vaz de Caminha, was arriving that day and I had gone to meet him on the quay at the head of a procession of friends, servants, boys and girls, all laughing and shouting as the arrival of a steamer was – indeed still is – a cause for great celebration.

The boat had already dropped anchor. With my telescope I could see Victorino on the deck waving towards the land. I recognized other faces too, mostly traders returning from holiday in Portugal. The exiles formed a group apart, huddled together like dogs and sniffing the air. I hated them. I was remembering with a sense of dread another evening (about which more later) when I suddenly noticed the figure of a white-haired old man with a very red face, tucked into a short jacket, with green and black checked trousers and patent leather shoes. Beside him was a tall, elegant man with a curling moustache, dressed all in white linen. I passed the telescope to my friend Irene Vandunem, the wife of the police chief, who prided herself on knowing all the gentlemen worth knowing who lived – or just passed through – Luanda. She had never seen him before. The two men came in on a launch, which stopped a few yards from the land, and completed their little journey carried on the sailors' backs. They passed us, wet, stunned, seeming to ignore the urchins' mocking laughter. Victorino came in on the second launch. Waving away the sailors' help he leapt into the water and ran up to greet us. Irene wanted to know at once whether he knew the two travellers. As I am sure you have already guessed, they were Carlos Fradique Mendes and his faithful Smith.

I saw Fradique again a month later at the Governor's Ball. He was speaking to Gabriela Santamarinha, a trader here, a base, malevolent creature, so ill-favoured in appearance and spirit that the people believe her to have been produced by a water-closet. That night Senhora Santamarinha looked rather like a turn-of-the-century cloud, a meringue, crammed into a long cream-coloured muslin and organdie dress with hoops and crinolines, covered in leaves and lace, her face powdered and her hair built up into a prodigy of capillary architecture. Fradique looked so frightened I could not help feeling sorry for him. I smiled at him, and he smiled back.

I knew that Arcénio Pompílio Pompeu de Carpo, then the possessor of one of the greatest fortunes in Luanda, had offered him lodging at his mansion. Arcénio was telling everybody that he had the last surviving Portuguese man 'from the Old Portugal' staying at his house. He swore blind that Fradique was an intimate friend of

Victor Hugo, that he had been with Garibaldi on his Sicil-
ian conquests, that just a few months back he had been in
Ethiopia, fighting on the side of Marshall Robert Napier's
Anglo-Indian expedition. What most impressed me was
learning that he had been with Bakunin in London in
1860, drinking vodka and discussing God and the State,
and listening to the great man's stories of how he had
escaped death in the icy camps of Siberia.

I asked Arcénio to introduce us. But as Carlos bent to
kiss my hand all I could think of to say – nervous as I was
– was to ask stupidly what he thought of Bakunin. He
looked at me, astonished. 'Don't tell me you're an anarchist?!' He laughed. He dropped his voice to a conspira-
torial whisper: 'If you're here with a plot to assassinate
the governor and blow up the palace you can count on my
full support.'

Victorino had no sympathy for him. He was irritated by
Fradique's fixed ideas, his scepticism, the facility with
which he theorized about all of the great troubles of
Angola though he was only newly arrived here. More than
anything he was irritated by what he himself called
Fradique's 'binding': the dress-coat perfectly tailored to
his body, the shirt without the tiniest stain, the black
pearl splendid in his shirt-front. He was almost offended
when I suggested that we invite him to dine with us:
'That thing isn't a man,' he muttered, 'he's a literary
invention.' I suspect he might have been jealous.

But notwithstanding (for Victorino never refused me
anything) Fradique did come for dinner two weeks later,
accompanied by the Arcénios de Carpo, father and son:
the former discreet as ever, the latter with his long waxed
moustache, dressed showily in striped trousers and a
very tight jacket which made him look longer and thinner
than ever. Everything about him gave off a strange scent,
warm and sweet, so intensely that one of my girls ran off

covering her nose. 'Savage!', young Arcénio cried after her. 'This perfume comes from France!'

In those days the Luanda night-time used to smell of *jinguba*, the peanut plant, since from that plant came the oil they used to light the streets. Fradique used to say that cities, like women, could be told apart by their smell. The ports of French west Africa smelled strongly of onions fried in butter (so he said), a concoction which the young people would rub on their bodies like a perfume; Rio de Janeiro smells of ripe guavas, Lisbon of sardines, basil and Members of Parliament. As Arcénio de Carpo (the elder) recalled, in the south of Angola, among the *cuamatos*, women rub their hair with cow dung, which for them is considered the most delicate of fragrances.

Fradique wanted to hear my opinion. I said that like the *buschmen* I preferred the simple scent of fresh rain to any perfume. Three months later I was sent a little lacquered crystal bottle containing water. On the label Fradique had written 'First autumn rain in Paris, October 20th, 1868.' Later, from a climb in the Alps he sent me the leavings of a storm; and in 1871 when he walked alone up the course of the Nile as far as the land of the Nubians, he gave me as a memento a few drops of dew gathered one gentle morning in Omdurman. This precious collection of rain, kept in more than fifty little bottles of all shapes and colours, crystal and porcelain, even includes a little holy water which fell one April evening over the Vatican; the melancholy drizzle of London from the day Victor Hugo died; and the salt mist of a storm at sea off Salvador, just after Fradique had said goodbye to me for the last time.

But all this was much later. Right now I want to tell you how I came to know him. That night at dinner we spoke about perfumes and about slavery, about the situation of traders in Angola and about the anarchist revolution. Fradique did not understand (he never could understand)

how Victorino could hold libertarian views and at the same
time defend Negro-trafficking. My husband explained (in
jest) that by sending Africans over to Brazil he was secretly
preparing for a revolution: 'The slaves make up the ferment
that will hasten the great insurrection. In the first place
because they are free spirits, not yet subjugated to the
monstrous idea of a God and a Paradise with which the
governments of Christian countries make a practice of
deceiving their people. It is in God – in the fiction of God –
that real slavery is to be found. Man will never be truly free
till he has eliminated Him. Voltaire used to say that you
could only demonstrate the existence of God by making
Him disappear. In the second place, because unlike European workers and countryfolk, Negroes do not really have
anything to lose. Revolution will break out in America and
Brazil, a revolution led by slaves, and it will spread across
the whole world.'

I'm sure he expected this to shock Fradique. But he
didn't succeed. 'There have always been slaves,' Fradique
said. 'And some, like Spartacus the Thracian, did organize
rebellions, but they were soon defeated and everything
went back to the way it had been before. That is the defi-
nition of a revolution: a complete rotation around an
immovable axis. But I agree with you about the death of
God. Satan, the first free thinker, incited man to disobey
God and eat the fruit of knowledge, and through this he
showed us the path to freedom. The problem is that man
is frightened by absolute freedom. That's all that the fable
of God and the Devil means.'

Two weeks after that dinner Victorino left Luanda for
Mossâmedes. He had (in his words) a cargo of freedom-
fighters to send to Brazil. A few days later I received a letter
from Fradique asking to see me, since he was planning a
trip to São Salvador do Congo and wanted my advice on
certain matters. I sent him a card telling him that he was

welcome to come. Although I was born in Luanda my mother taught me to speak the language of the Congo and of the Cabindans, and I visited my parents' land many times – as a result it was not (still is not) unusual for bush-traders and adventurers, whether Portuguese or not, to seek me out when planning to travel on land beyond Ambriz.

I received him in the library. I wanted to show him a rare collection of maps (which, alas, were lost when I fled to Brazil in 1875), showing the occupation of the Congo over the last two centuries and the way in which the shape of that region has been changing. Fradique took an interest in the maps. He told me that he was planning to study the ruins of São Salvador, once the capital of one of the most powerful kingdoms in Africa, and whose churches and buildings (apparently) combine European and indigenous skills in an architecture which is something quite new.

We were both bent over the maps. All of a sudden Fradique raised his eyes to meet mine. He laughed: 'Young Arcénio is crazy about you,' he said. I didn't know how to answer him. I had been aware of Arcénio's interest for some time. At parties he would watch me, solemnly, as I danced. He would greet me too formally when we met in the street. Once my friend Irene brought me a letter from him. It was a love poem, a bad one, which I read and tore up. Irene was angry with me: 'even dirty water can put out a fire' she pronounced in quimbundu.

Fradique looked intensely at me. 'You are the proof that God exists,' he said, 'and that he is quite mad'. He leaned towards me and kissed me, and I kissed him. Later we went back to looking at the maps, and played a game of chess. I asked him what he had meant when he spoke about God's madness. Fradique laughed. 'Only a thoroughly insane God could conceive of an angel, and then place her in Hell.'

The following week Fradique left for São Salvador do Congo, and from there travelled to Cabinda where he boarded a brig bound for Lisbon. I did not see him again until 1872. Victorino had died two years earlier, drowned in the Quanza when one of his pilot-boats overladen with barrels of *cachaça* capsized off Feira do Dondo. He had always felt sure that alcohol would kill him in the end, just as it did.

Victorino's death left me in a state of total collapse for many weeks. When I did at last recover I found to my surprise that I had become overnight one of the richest people in the country. I sold the ships my husband had used to make his fortune, I bought lands at the mouth of the Loge and the Quanza, in Malange and Icolo e Bengo, and took advantage of my good relations with the people of the north to set up trading posts in Mazamandombe, Cabeça da Cobra and Mangue Pequeno, very close to Santo Antonio of Zaïre.

When he next disembarked, back in Luanda, Fradique found me dressed in my black *nga muturi* (widow's clothes), doing the accounts for the wax and ivory, salt and *cachaça*, organizing caravans, negotiating with *pombeiros* and hawkers, all this (as you can imagine) utterly terrified, young and inexperienced as I was.

Fradique had come over on this occasion in an attempt to solve a little mystery. When he had visited São Salvador five years earlier he met an old trader by the name of Quissongo (whom I also knew) with many years' experience in the bush and an inexhaustible supply of fantastic stories. Quissongo had shown him the travel-journal of an Italian adventurer, Carlo Esmeraldi, who had been a friend of his, who had disappeared some time before, somewhere in the backwoods of Benguela. Quissongo said that the journal had been given to him by one of the luggage-bearers on Esmeraldi's expedition. This man was suffering from *hoxa* (the name given around here to sleeping sickness, trypanosomiasis, the illness resulting from the bite of the tsetse fly), and was almost unrecognizable, thin and dirty, his body covered in sores, sinking into overwhelming sleeps from which he would wake only to beg for fresh water or to cry out incoherently.

Esmeraldi's diary, which Fradique bought for the price of an ox, is (I still have it) extemely peculiar. The writing of the first entries, small, regular, even elegant, is transformed bit by bit as Esmeraldi gets deeper into the bush (and into the even more distant recesses of his own soul) into dispersed, confused scrawlings, and where at the start he has written only in Italian, by the end he is mixing it with delirious observations in French and even Portuguese. This change takes place around the second month of his trip, near a place in the interior where Esmeraldi claims to have discovered intact the prow of a tall ship. 'I am deeply impressed,' the adventurer writes. 'Who could have brought this object here? And how could they have brought it? And whatever for?' He then explains that is it a large, solid prow, with at its centre the enigmatic figure of a *kabeiros*, the phallic demon worshipped in ancient Samothrace and believed to be the protector of sailors and navigators. 'So many miles from the coast,' Esmeraldi writes on, 'the inexplicable presence of this object is quite a challenge to the imagination'.

From this point his writing begins to get more nervous, there are gaps in the text, torn pages, and the meaning of phrases begin to get lost in the profusion of disconnected observations. Esmeraldi denounces repeatedly, obsessively, the existence of what he calls geological aberrations: 'There are geological aberrations, errors in the construction of the world. What dangerous prodigies may be hidden at the heart of mountains?' And then 'At this place where I am now there are no birds in the sky. The big trees curve towards the west and if we throw a stone up vertically we can see it describe an ellipse, also falling towards that same direction. Two days' journey from this place we uncoupled a heavy Boer cart from its oxen and it rolled up a hill with a 14-degree gradient!'

The style of his writing worsens over the last pages. 'Don't ask me for names. In this damned place all names are damned, and besides none of the maps know them. Here the earth devours itself. I don't imagine a fissure at the bottom of the ravine, I imagine a mouth!'

I think (but this is just a suspicion) that he was suffering from *hoxa*. That was what I said to Fradique when he showed me the diary for the first time. But our friend did not listen to me. He believed that the Italian really had discovered some strange natural phenomenon.

'All the bearers have abandoned me, save only one,' Esmeraldi wrote later. 'Today I'm going down alone to the bottom of the ravine. I know that what awaits me there will not be the entrance to Hades. A gravitational aberration such as this could be explained by the presence at the bottom of the fissure of some mass of great density. Perhaps a meteorite has fallen here, some rock which is not necessarily very large but which is very, very heavy. So dense and so heavy that it is capable of attracting anything close to it, increasing its weight and density still further.'

Fradique wanted to retrace Esmeraldi's route based on the information recorded in the diary. He just laughed when I tried to dissuade him. 'One day', he said, 'the King of the Butterflies sent an emissary to discover the nature of fire. Some time later the emissary returned, saying that he had discovered fire, that he had found it a volatile, enraged substance, and that he had been too afraid to get any closer. So a second emissary set off, who soon returned exhausted, half mad, his wings singed, but the King was still not satisfied and sent his own son off, telling him not to return until he had discovered what fire really is. The son set off, but never returned. The King was satisfied – his son *had* discovered the true nature of fire.'

Fortunately Fradique fell ill with malaria in Benguela, and was unable to continue his journey. When he returned to Luanda he was thin, downcast, but still ready to try his luck at some other time. It was August. In the five months that followed I was happy, and I think Fradique was too. I can now see that those days divided my life into two halves. When I think of the past, it falls into the before and the after. Before, I was a child, and did not know what happiness was; after, I lost my innocence, and would never be able to be happy again.

I remember myself as a young girl visiting my father in prison. We would see him there most Sundays, sitting in a chair, on the patio of the fort, wearing his military jacket and a piece of cloth tied around his waist, his right hand holding a thick wooden walking-stick. Dozens of people visited him, people who would come from the Congo especially to see him, and for me it was always a kind of party – there was always singing and dancing, and I was a girl who loved to sing and dance.

One foggy morning my father died – I'll never forget it; that night the drumming kept everybody awake, and the same happened the following night. The old ladies convulsed as though possessed by some foreign spirit and wailed like madwomen as I passed them. The white men were getting nervous. One evening a group of exiles approached my mother and I on the Calçada dos Enforcados, and while two of them held me back the others ripped off her clothes right there, beat and kicked her, finally leaving her for dead, lying out face down in the dust.

Someone went running to fetch Victorino. He soon arrived at the head of a group of *cuamato* slaves, very tall, very dangerous men, all carrying spears, machetes and old fowling-pieces, and shouting, jumping, singing, as if they were off to war. 'Let's kill them all,' Victorino said, shooing away the old ladies and children who had gathered around us. He gave orders for my mother to be placed in a litter and carried home; then he drew his gun from his belt, went back to the group of men and together they began to make their way down the hill.

The exiles were in a tavern belonging to a Galician very close by, celebrating what they had done. As they noticed the arrival of the posse one managed to escape – I can see him now, running like the devil from the *cuamatos*, children and dogs, flying off around the back of the hayfields, until at last he reached the fort. Meanwhile the others had barricaded themselves in the tavern and were responding to the siege with gunfire. Victorino spread his men around the road, behind trees and walls, and shouted to the children to leave.

The *cuamatos* were terribly excited, making an enormous din – it was just as if they had returned to the savannahs of the south. All of a sudden one of them dashed out towards the tavern, embedded his spear in the door, and ran back as quickly as he had gone. Then another did the same, and a third, and this was what was going on when the figure of the Chief of Police appeared at the end of the road, Major Cristiano Pereira do Santos Vandunem, a man so used to holding positions of authority that it used to be said of him that he could light a cigar merely by ordering it to light itself.

Vandunem walked slowly up the road, accompanied by two corporals just as black as him, one on each side, and he did not draw his gun until he was just a few metres from the tavern. 'Your Excellency,' he shouted to Victorino. 'Do me a favour and go home – you have already caused me enough trouble today.' He yanked the spears out of the door, and with a firm kick knocked it down. He put the gun back in his belt, went inside, and returned with the exiles slapping them about like naughty little schoolboys.

It was on that day that Victorino first noticed me. Until then it had been as if I hadn't existed. But from then on he began to tell me apart from the other children, and when I turned ten he asked my mother to let me attend a little school in Caponta which he himself had had built for the children of his servants. The teacher, a young priest called Nicolau dos Anjos, who later became well known as a magician and a miracle-worker, was a tiny little man, so small that even among the pygmies he would have been considered a dwarf. Any of his students, any child at all, was taller than him, but this didn't diminish his authority one bit.

Victorino and the priest felt a respectful hatred towards each other. Perhaps I should explain myself: the priest hated Victorino for mocking the church, for reading Proudhon and Baudelaire, for swearing that he hoped yet to be able to strangle the very last priest in the world with the guts of the very last bourgeois. On the other hand he did admire his courage, his strength of character, the fact that he always took the side of the Angolans, the blacks and the mestizos in any conflict with the Portuguese.

Meanwhile Victorino hated the priest simply because he wore a cassock, and even more because he was a Bonapartist, a reactionary, and a sworn enemy of the naturalist movement in literature. At the same time he valued his love of his fellow-man, his detachment from earthly things, the fervour with which he devoted himself to educating the people. Their mutual hatred, but a hatred cultivated with civility and affability, was something which everyone around them found quite disconcerting, and was the subject of numerous anecdotes going around the city.

You must want to know why I married Victorino. The answer is simple: because he made me feel loved (and protected). It's true that at first I was afraid of him, of his long prophet's beard and his inflamed look, his stormy past and his sudden rages. But then, bit by bit, I began to allow myself to be seduced by the overwhelming torrent of that belated passion. Victorino was proud of the hawkers' rhetoric he used to astonish strangers, as he related stories of impossible adventures, of voyages he had never taken, of meetings he had never had, and in truth at that time his words conquered me too.

I enjoyed visiting him in the library to listen to him talking about books. The library was set up in a high-ceilinged, spacious hall, its walls covered in solid mahogany bookcases. There was a little gallery running all around it, supported by columns, in order to allow access to the higher shelves. Victorino had had a dome-shaped window opened in the roof, which had a mechanism by which it could be opened or closed. When I visited him there I would sit and look at the spines of the books lined up on the shelves, trying to decipher the titles, many of them in languages I did not know, and dreaming of foreign lands. Victorino hung hammocks between the columns, magnificent sleeping-hammocks with elaborate borders, and would leave the books he was reading on them. Thus decorated, the library seemed like a ship, one of those that travels down the Amazon laden with rubber, with parrots and Indians, between Manaus and Belém do Pará.

Lying on one of the hammocks I would watch the dusk settling, the golden light falling on the books, I would hear dogs barking in the distance, and then see the sky turn dark, and deep, and soon it would be covered with star-dust. Stars and books. The universe, the unknown, was right there, all around me, and Victorino was the only person who could open the doors to that world – to The World – for me.

I suspect our marriage shocked a lot of people. Nicolau dos Anjos refused to conduct the ceremony (at the time I did not understand why) and instead it was a parish priest from Braga, a little, round, red-faced man who couldn't pronounce his 'r's, who – as they say – united us in the holy bonds of matrimony.

The whole of Luanda was invited to the *quizomba* (that is the name we give in this country to an important party). A delegation came from the Congo, with dancers and drummers, five oxen, a huge elephant tusk, pigs, goats, chickens, a great deal of fruit and other foodstuffs. From Salvador da Bahia came a mysterious old man whom Victorino introduced to me (to my surprise) as his old Teacher, who left just as he had arrived; from the interior of the country there came *pombeiros*, businessmen, people for whom Victorino was a kind of God. For two days and two nights this whole crowd drank, ate and danced, until Victorino – fed up with the noise – ordered the remaining food and drink to be distributed in the outskirts of the town, and bade the guests farewell.

My husband always treated me like a princess; he opened the doors to the world to me, he taught me what he knew of literature and the arts. Anything I desired, anything attainable, was mine for the asking. A few months after the wedding he had a young Frenchman sent over from Paris, François de Bigault, to teach me the language. François disembarked here with a chest full of books, and it did not take him long to stir up the whole town, since besides being a teacher he was also an artist

(more or less), and among Luanda's ladies there was
great demand for his services, either to help them to read
Balzac in the original or to sit to him for their portraits (or
indeed both).

Irene Vandunem was one of those who had her portrait
done, in her drawing-room, with a monkey asleep on her
lap and two girls at her feet. Her husband did not like the
picture and turned up at our house, dressed as though he
were on his way to a funeral. 'Your Excellency,' he said to
Victorino, 'take care with that guest of yours, the Frenchman. There are many people in this town who do not
wish him well.' François left the following morning,
almost in secret, on a caravan that was bound for
Quiloango, and from there boarded a boat for Lisbon. A
few months after his departure, four of my slavegirls gave
birth to mestizo children, three boys and a girl, all of
them healthy and happy, all of them with the beautiful
slim face and almond eyes of François. The same happened in other houses too. And to this day, even so many
years on, François is still remembered in Luanda, and
whenever a man abandons his duty and runs off, leaving
a woman expecting a child, people will say 'So-and-so has
gone *à la française*'.

Later Victorino brought a piano teacher back from
Naples for me. He was an equally flamboyant man, but
(to calm the fears of the heads of the families here) rather
more flamboyant than men in our society habitually are.
He would wear long silk bows in preposterous colours,
costume waistcoats, white gloves even during the rainy
season; he would appear for lunch every day wrapped in
a velvet dressing-gown, waving a peacock-feather fan,
making delicate complaints about the intolerable African
heat. Unlikely as this may sound he was called Angelo de
la Morte, but the natives soon gave him another name,
Ohali, the Crested Grebe, and that was how he became

known throughout this city, throughout our São Paolo da Assunção de Luanda.

With Ohali I learnt to transpose a few little Angolan *modas* for the piano, tunes which Fradique liked very much. I came across two or three of these songs again, later, with other words and different arrangements, by which time they had become great successes at the carnival dances in Recife and Rio de Janeiro. Ohali also taught me the modern art of photography which he practised rather more profitably than he did music. In 1887, when I visited Paris for the first time, my collection of prints of the Congo greatly impressed Felix Tournachon (Nadar), to whom I was introduced at a party at the house of Madame de Jouarre.

But let us get back to August 1872. I was saying that those months that followed Fradique's return from Benguela were the happiest of my life. In a way I imagine eternity must be a little like a photograph (a place without time) of the good and bad times we have lived through. And thus, for eternity, we will be living through them for ever, Hell and Heaven at once. Those months I lived beside Fradique will be my Heaven, the time I lived as a slave to Gabriela Santamarinha my Hell.

Once Fradique asked me why I didn't free my slaves. I explained to him that they had been brought up with me, under my roof, that I felt attached to them as though they were my own family (and besides we do indeed all use the same surname). And I quoted the Bible: 'It may be that thy bondman will say unto thee 'I will not go away from thee', because he loveth thee and thine house, because he is well with thee; then thou shalt take an awl, and thrust it through his ear unto the door, and he shall be thy servant for ever.' (Deut. 15)

Irritated, Fradique asked me what I felt, I who was the daughter of a slave and who had been a slave myself. What answer could I give? If he had asked me the same question today, I would have answered with the Creole proverb from Sierra Leone, a country I recently visited: *stone we dei botam wata, no say wen rain de cam*; in other words, a stone underwater doesn't know when it is raining.

As a rule the city slave pays no attention to what it means not to be a slave, or at least doesn't waste his time dreaming up philosophies about it. He works (since he is obliged to do this), he eats, he drinks and he sleeps. I was only aware of what it was not to be free when, after having been mistress to a number of slaves, I returned (in the most brutal way) to that condition myself.

It is still painful for me to talk about it. It all happened like a nightmare. On the 26th of May, 1876, I was one of the richest and most respected people in Angola. I owned properties in the city and in the outskirts, oxen, I had an income and a large household. I was received in the Governor's Palace almost every week to discuss matters of trade and local administration; I chaired various committees, I had my own seat at the Providência Theatre. The next day an adventurer came into my house, accompanied by the chief of police (my friend), slapped me across the face, and at that moment I learnt that I was his slave.

This adventurer, whose name I refuse to pronounce out of a sense of decency and propriety, had arrived in Luanda as a fugitive, not a thing to his name but an Indian he had brought to serve him. As he was Victorino's brother I welcomed him into my house, I lent him money, I introduced him to the most influential people in the city. Within two or three weeks he was already plotting against me, calling into question my honour and my honesty, doubting whether I was capable of managing the fortune Victorino had left me. Finally, on the night when – in front of our guests – he raised his voice to insult me, I had him whipped out of the house.

Three weeks later I was his slave. I won't bore you with explanations of the legal tricks that allowed this crime to take place (all you need know is that out of carelessness, and owing to the unexpectedness of his death, Victorino had died without filling out my freedom papers, nor did he leave a will). So all at once I found myself dispossessed of everything that I had so lately called mine – including myself.

My mother died in June, disgusted to see me in that situation and with no wish to see the worst of it. She had been with me when that criminal burst into our house, accompanied by Cristiano Pereira dos Santos Vandunem, the Chief of Police, and struck me; I screamed that I would kill him, and I would have done it too (I was holding a gun) if my mother hadn't intervened. Cristiano held the villain by the arm and told him that while he did have some rights over me he had no right to mistreat me. Although he said this without raising his voice, it was as though he had bitten him.

I learnt later that Arcénio de Carpo had also sent him an extremely violent letter (written in words I could not possibly repeat here) and it may be that all this did prevent him from going even further. After my mother's death he came to see me in my room, and without raising his eyes to meet mine, told me that he had decided to employ me in the service of Gabriela Santamarinha. It was a trick to rid himself of me, of all that I represented, but at the same time a cruel vengeance too, for he knew well how Gabriela hated me.

Sometimes I think of Evil as being like an animal. An Austrian friend of mine, who spent many months in Angola studying the exotic fauna and flora of the bush-lands of the South, maintained that an anthill (or a bee-hive) can be seen as a single living being, where each ant (or bee) is a cell. In just the same way I imagine Evil as a vast, dispersed animal, spread all over the world, composed of people in just the same way as an anthill is made up of ants. Even without knowing each other, they *do* know each other, they act in unison, all moving in the same direction.

I feel this about Gabriela Santamarinha and the other man – the Bahian – whom I refuse to name. The two of them met (or perhaps, 'recognized each other' would be better) at a carnival party, where he was dressed as an Arab, she as a woman from Spain. From then on their hatred was united in all manner of schemes, against me on some occasions, or simply against anyone in Luanda who seemed to them to be happy. Gabriela abhorred other people's happiness, just as nature abhors a vacuum. The laughter of a child, a young man's smile, irritated and offended her. But the thing she could not abide was requited love. My relationship with Fradique drove her insane.

In this city intrigue is a kind of game, played everywhere, by rich and poor, with great enthusiasm; this made it a most propitious climate for the development of Senhora Santamarinha's demented imagination, her talent for slander and lies. From an innocent phrase overheard accidentally on the street she was able to construct conspiracies, to imagine intrigues, to contrive a whole, sordid universe.

I still have no notion of how she came to know about my relationship with Fradique; indeed she probably didn't know it, she just imagined it. What is certain is that even while my husband was alive she was already spreading word about the city that I meant to run off with the 'Little Nobleman', as she called him, and later that I *had* actually run off with him. Victorino began to receive anonymous letters (which were not really anonymous – the style was unmistakable); these he read with enthusiasm, as he had been fascinated by monstrosities all his life. It was a passion that had led him to assemble a collection of inexplicable objects, things that were meaningless or simply repugnant, which he meant to use to demonstrate God's irresponsibility (or alternatively His non-existence). He considered Gabriela's letters, in their wickedness and incoherence, to be of just the same nature as a lizard with two heads.

Later, when Fradique visited Luanda for the second time, Gabriela Damned-Mouth (as the people called her) swore to Irene Vandunem that he had tried to seduce her (!). The virtuous Gabriela had fought off the advances of the 'Little Nobleman', shouting to her girls for help. Soon after that, when Fradique returned from Benguela (convalescing from an attack of malaria) she accused me of having bewitched him. This was not the first time she had accused me of such things; by her logic, since my father had been from the Congo and as such was adept in witchcraft, then surely I must have been a witch too.

One evening, when I had at last grown tired of these fantasies, I went to her house to speak to her. I found her in the sewing-room, training her monkeys to dance the *rebita* – besides tormenting her slaves this was all she ever did. As she saw me arrive she approached me with open arms, calling me 'cousin' (as friends here often address each other) and inviting me to sit down. I told her there was no need: 'What I have to say would best be said standing, and right away, since afterwards I am sure you are not going to want me to stay.' I told her that if she persisted in embroiling my name in her imaginary dramas, I would have my servants come over and wash out her mouth with turpentine. The poor woman turned ashen, stammered something, rolled her eyes and finally disappeared – shrieking – into the house.

I did not see her again until the day my Hell began. She came to collect me, with her court of white and albino servants. 'My dear friend!' she cried, looking at me slowly, sadly, as though she was truly sorry for the situation: 'That's life: you light a fire in the morning, and at night it consumes you.'

My household, alarmed at the events of the recent days, did not want to let me leave. Like me, they couldn't understand what was happening. Many were in tears. I told them not to worry, that it was my house, that I would soon be returning.

Gabriela Santamarinha lived in a big old house on the Rua dos Mercadores, a building with thick walls which had once served as a police headquarters. In the cellar there was a little dungeon that had been converted into a store-room, and it was there that I was taken. I was left alone there for the first night, but the next morning one of the slaves, Júlia, a native of Rio de Janeiro, was sent down to keep me company. She showed me where her back was cut from lashes of Gabriela's whip. 'She will whip you too,' she said. The certainty that I was to be submitted to the same torture seemed to make her happy.

I spent a week locked up in those conditions. I lay on the damp mat, struggling to breathe the mossy air, and bit by bit I came to feel as though I were sinking into a dark, dreamless sleep, which was one way of trying to forget my fear and my shame. Júlia would bring my food and make me eat as she told me the latest news: whom Gabriela had beaten that evening, what was being said about me around the city, how the damned Bahian was squandering Victorino's fortune.

One night I awoke with the sensation that something darker than mere darkness had entered my cell. I couldn't make out any outline, nor could I hear any sound, not even the slightest whisper; but I could feel the warmth of a body very close to me, an evil presence, someone watching me from beyond the shadows. I was at the bottom of a well, alone with a serpent. 'You people can take every-thing from me,' I murmured, 'but I will always have more than you.' She did not speak. She got up, and left.

Júlia appeared very early the next morning, rosy-cheeked with excitement: 'The Mistress is planning a party, and she wants you to help us in the kitchen.' A party? Gabriela Damned-Mouth clearly meant to show off my disgrace. I smiled at Júlia: 'Tell your mistress that I'm not leaving this room.' Moments later Gabriela appeared, enraged, with two of her servants, and I was dragged up to the yard, stripped, tied to a hook on the wall and whipped.

The party took place that night. From my cell, burning with fever, I heard Júlia playing the piano, I heard voices and laughter. They were just upstairs, all those people who had frequented my house so recently, those old friends of Victorino, the cream of Luandan society.

In the few weeks that followed I was terribly sick. Even now I have difficulty putting the events of that time into order. I remember that one of the albino girls came to find me in a panic to deliver a letter to me, the letter Fradique had written me from Lisbon. I remember this as though it were a part of a dream. One day (one night?) I heard shouts and a man I knew well, a servant of Arcénio de Carpo, appeared in my cell, a torch in his left hand and a rifle in his right. You know the rest.

Many people are unable to understand why most slaves accept their lot once they have arrived in America or Brazil. At the time I didn't understand it either. Now I do. On board the ship on which we fled Angola, the *Nação Crioula*, I met an old man who claimed to have been a friend of my father. He reminded me that in our language (as in almost all West African languages) the same word is used for 'the sea' and 'death': *Calunga*. So for most slaves that journey was a passage across death. The life they had left behind in Africa was Life; the one they found in America or Brazil, a Rebirth.

It was just so for me too. In Pernambuco, and later in Bahia, I was reborn, slowly, as a new woman. Sometimes I would be visited by the memory of some face, the figure of someone I had loved and whom I had left in Luanda, but to whom I could not put a name. I thought of my friends as characters of a book I had read. Angola was a personal sickness, a vague, indefinite pain, throbbing in some remote corner of my soul.

By the time Sophia was born I already felt Brazilian; although whenever I heard someone singing those simple lines from the mulatto poet Antonio Gonçalves Dias lamenting his *saudades* for Brazil – 'Oh my land has palm trees growing / Where we heard the thrushes' song / All the songbirds singing here / Will never sing like those back home' – whenever I heard those lines it was Angola that I would think of: 'Oh my land has its perfections / Which here cannot be found / Oh God, don't let me die / Till I'm back home in my land'. In 1889, just a few months after Fradique's death, I heard those lines being sung again, and I knew that I had to return to Luanda. I sold the Cajaíba Plantation which Fradique had left me, and set off with our daughter and one servant.

As you doubtless know, Gonçalves Dias disappeared on his trip back to Brazil, when the ship carrying him, the *Ville de Boulogne*, was wrecked somewhere in the mid-Atlantic. I was luckier – my ship survived; but I found Angola on the verge of a wreck itself. The total elimination of slaving in the Portuguese colonies, and the subsequent declaration of the Lei Áurea, the Abolition Law, had damaged the old families. Most of my friends received me with suspicion. They did not understand why I had returned, and still do not.

At the dock Arcénio Pompílio Pompeu de Carpo was waiting for us. He had come back to Luanda five years earlier, intending once again to kill the man who had murdered his father; but no sooner had he disembarked in Luanda than he learned that he had come too late – the man who had caused all our miseries had died, laughing, as he sat telling anecdotes, surrounded by his friends.

As for Gabriela Damned-Mouth, I found her in ruins. Insane, almost always the worse for drink, she wandered the streets, screaming. Children threw stones at her, dogs barked as she passed. Then I stopped hearing of her, until a couple of weeks ago when father Nicolau dos Anjos, on a visit to Luanda, told me that he had seen her in Dondo, selling vegetables and roasted rats.

So now you know my story, or at least most of it. You might be interested to know that I married Arcénio de Carpo. I am happy, in the way that people tend to be happy. I live my life as though sitting on a verandah – I watch people pass by in the streets, people with their own intimate tragedies. I watch them being born and dying. Even nature herself conspires against us in this acidic place; a man dies, disappears, and before long everything he created is corroded, corrupted, and breaks apart. Today's palaces will be tomorrow's ruins. Here a pan of soup left out in the open will ferment overnight. Fungi grow like malignant plants in our cupboards, and if we only let them they would take over our whole rooms, our houses. Even memory dissolves quickly. I don't think anyone here still remembers how old Arcénio de Carpo died; still less do they remember Fradique Mendes. They call me 'the Brazilian woman', and the younger among them actually believe that I was born in Brazil. That is another reason why I am sending you these letters. Do with them as you see fit.

From one who admires you greatly,
though from far away,
Ana Olímpia